# Burden

## Dark Wolves Series book 4

By

## Élianne Adams

Cover Art by Jacqueline Sweet Design


Paperback ISBN 978-1-988644-02-8

# Other Titles by Élianne Adams

## Return to Avalore Series
Flickering Light
Call of the Dragon
Rise of the Phoenix
Once Upon a Fiery Christmas
Lost in Magic

## Dragon Blood Series
Releasing Her Dragon
Her Gingerbread Dragon
Finding His Dragon
His Secret Dragon
Saving His Dragon
Keeping His Dragon (Fall 2017)

## Dark Wolves Series
Torment
Betrayal
Wrath
Burden

## Sugar Shack Series
Northern Sass
Candy Sass (November 2017)

**Deadly Whispers Series**
Bump in the Night
Fallen Angel

**Single Titles**
Black Velvet
Burn Deep

# Coming Soon!

**Mates of the Citadel Series**
Damon (Fall 2017)
Axton
Keilon

# Burden

Elianne Adams

http://elianneadams.com/

BURDEN · 2

# « CHAPTER 1 »

Joss's entire body shook with the growls he barely contained. After all the Mahehkans had done to his pack—to his family—he had thought no amount of depravity would shock him. He'd been wrong.

Unable to turn away, Joss watched the beautiful young she-wolf sleep. Her long black hair covered his pillow like delicate lace. Her breaths, slow and deep, slipped from her parted lips. She looked so at peace, so serene, he could almost pretend they hadn't hurt her. *Damn those bastards.*

Even though they had returned to the Komoro village three days earlier, she had yet to speak a single word. *Violet.* The only reason he knew his mate's name is because Delana had asked one of the other women they had rescued who she was. Weak and malnourished, Violet spent most of her time sleeping or sipping the herbal tea Delana brought her every morning.

Violet groaned and turned onto her back, bringing her right hand up to her belly. Even in sleep, she grimaced. He took a quick step forward. His wolf beat at him, trying to get to her. It wanted to soothe and comfort her, but Violet was nowhere near ready for that.

She didn't open her eyes, but her fluttering eyelids gave her away. Joss's gaze drifted to her temple where the dark purple bruise was slowly fading. As a wolf shifter, the injury should have healed within hours—a day at most. So either her injury was more severe than he'd suspected, or her wolf had given up. Neither option was a good one.

The growl he'd suppressed since he'd entered the room rumbled free.

Joss flinched at the small whimper that came from the she-wolf in his bed. He would rather cut off each of his limbs than harm a single hair on her beautiful head, but she didn't know that. "I know you're awake, Violet." The smell of her fear assaulted him for what seemed like the hundredth time since he'd brought her home. Maybe he should have let her go to one of his pack sister's homes while she recuperated, but just the thought of her being anywhere but with him made his wolf furious. It needed to keep watch. To protect.

"Delana says you can eat today. I've prepared some things I thought you might like," he told her as he crossed the room and placed the tray next to her on the bed. Her nostrils flared, and her eyes slit open, but she made no other move. She didn't even look to be breathing.

"Listen, I know you're scared—you have every right to be—but you're safe here."

She opened her eyes wider and gasped when he sat on the edge of the bed. The distress and mistrust dulling them gutted him, but in time, she'd learn her past was truly that, in the past. The last thing he wanted to do was push her to do anything, but too much was at stake. Today, his only goal was to get her to eat. No matter what.

"There's nothing wrong with the food I've brought you. I'll even taste it myself to prove it, but then I expect you to have some. The baby needs more than herbal tea to grow and be healthy."

Violet looked at him, then at the food. Her eyes shone with tears she had yet to release, at least not in his presence. With a long, shaky breath, she sat up as far away from him on the other side of the bed as she could and nodded.

Joss's heart pounded. All his other attempts at communication when she'd woken had resulted in one huge failure after another. One little nod from her, and he was ready to smile and shout from the rooftops. It was a small gesture, hardly anything at all, but for her, it was huge.

He plucked a piece of dried meat from the tray and popped it into his mouth. He didn't fail to notice that Violet swallowed when he did. She had to be hungry. When he finished, he opened up and showed her the food was gone. "Do you need me to try the berries and the cheese, as well?"

He didn't expect her trust. Not yet. She'd been through too much. And asking her to make decisions, as small as they were, put the power back in her control. He had a feeling she hadn't had a whole lot of either in a long time.

Her mouth opened and for a half second, he thought he might finally get to hear his mate's voice, but then she snapped it shut and tilted her chin up before nodding again.

Joss swallowed his disappointment. At least she was looking at him today. It was progress. He ate a berry, then a piece of cheddar, showing her once again that he'd swallowed what he'd taken. Some of the women had told Delana that they had been fed rancid food on a regular basis. It was no wonder they didn't trust even the most basic thing—a good meal.

"I've always loved the preserves more than anything else," he told her before pulling it out and sticking the treat into his mouth. "My sister makes the best jam."

Joss slid the tray closer to her and waited. He didn't want to be pushy, but for the baby's sake, he'd get her to eat.

She glanced at the tray and licked her lips. Pulling her long black hair over her left shoulder, she exposed more of the bruising on her neck. A bite mark. Each time he'd seen it, his wolf had raged. Its fury beat at him so hard that his skin prickled with the need to shift, but he shoved the beast back. He took a slow breath through his nose, trying his damnedest to keep his growl deep inside. The tips of his fingers burned as his claws fought to break through the skin.

Violet's eyes rounded, and her hands fisted on her thighs.

"It's okay. You're safe here." He would keep repeating the words until she believed them.

She waited so long before unfurling her fingers and reaching for the food that he was afraid she wouldn't. Keeping her gaze locked on him, she blindly grabbed some cheese. When she finally got it close to her mouth, her hand trembled so hard that it fell from her fingers, bouncing off the mattress and onto the floor.

A strangled sound came from Violet's throat, and she sank further from him. Her eyes watered, and her bottom lip wobbled.

*Jesus.* What the hell had they put her through that such a small mishap would cause such a visceral reaction? The scent of her fear, which had yet to dissipate fully, intensified to the point of making his nose itch with the effort to keep from sneezing.

"That piece wasn't good enough for you, anyway. Clearly, I cut it crooked or something for it to go flying out of your fingers like that." He'd tried being serious and being calm. Neither had worked. Maybe if he kidded with her a bit, she would loosen up.

Her eyebrows rose a touch, but otherwise, she kept looking at him with a wary gaze and her fingers clutched in front of her belly. As much as he wanted to be near her, he couldn't. She—and the baby— needed nourishment. She was way too thin. "If you promise to eat, I'll leave you alone so you won't be so afraid, but the little one needs food. Can you do that?"

He waited for her tiny nod before standing and crossing to the open bedroom door. He glanced at her over his shoulder, smiling when he found her with a strawberry already in her hand.

Her cheeks flushed and she immediately cast her gaze down to the comforter. The progress was slow, but it was there. She'd be okay. Eventually.

## « CHAPTER 2 »

Violet's stomach rumbled so hard she was amazed her mate hadn't come running back in to check on her. *Her mate.* Why now, when she could never accept his claim—provided he even wanted to claim her—did he have to come into her life? It was bad enough that her panic overwhelmed her to the point of feeling lightheaded each time he came near, but she was carrying another male's baby. One, no matter what the circumstances of his or her conception, she intended to raise and love as every child deserved.

She eyed the food on the tray and examined the strawberry still clutched between her fingers. Everything looked delicious. The meat smelled like heaven, and she couldn't remember the last time she even had cheese. She hardly knew where to start. Protein. The baby needed protein. And lots of vitamins. But the preserves made her mouth water. He hadn't tasted the bread, but he would have, had she asked. There was an honesty in his eyes that even she couldn't deny. She reached for a roll and broke a small piece. She closed her eyes to savor the taste. It was so soft it all but melted in her mouth. Her belly grumbled again.

As much as she wanted the sweet jam, there was no way her stomach would handle a lot of food. She had to do what was right for the baby. Once she started, it didn't take long for her stomach to fill with the berries and meat. She eyed the bread and preserves again, but there just wasn't any room. Anything more and she'd make herself sick. She sighed and stood, placing the tray on the dresser closest to the door.

She listened for movement outside before pulling the top drawer open. A fresh wave of Joss's scent billowed from it. She picked up the T-shirt at the top, careful not to unfold it or wrinkle it, and brought it up to her nose. She'd done the same thing a few times, and each time she had, her wolf had perked up a little. Not much, but enough to let her know that she wasn't completely gone.

Violet scanned the room. Maybe she could find a spot to hide a roll or two for later. She listened for noise on the other side of the door again. When all was silent, she grabbed two of the soft buns. She couldn't put them in the drawers. He'd find them there for sure. Maybe behind the bed? She dismissed that idea just as quickly. Damn it, it didn't matter where she hid them, he'd sniff them out in seconds with his wolf's nose.

A huge lump formed in her throat. She'd been reduced to hoarding food? Stashing it so that she could find it again later? She shook her head and placed the bread back on the tray. Her vision blurred, and as hard as she tried to blink the tears away, they streamed down her cheeks. A small sob rose up her throat, trying to choke her.

Footsteps approached on the other side of the door. Violet's heart pounded, and her breath caught in her lungs. Everything inside her screamed to run, to get away. She took a step back, then another until her knees touched the mattress behind her. She shimmied around it until she was on the other side of the bed. By the time the door swung open, she'd backed herself into the corner against the far wall.

"Are you okay?" Joss asked her from the doorway. The color drained from his face as he glanced to where she was clutching her belly. "Is it the baby? Was the food too much?"

Joss stepped into the room, his movements smooth as he crossed over to her. Worry and determination fought for dominance on his expressive face.

"I heard you crying. Are you in pain? I can ask Delana to get something for you," he finally said when he'd reached her.

Violet dropped her gaze to the floor, silently cursing herself for the reaction. Before Roger's reign of terror, she would have proudly called herself an Omega, but her old Mahehkan Alpha and his dirtbag followers had turned her into something she was not. A cowering shell of her former self. How could she hope that anyone else would respect her when she couldn't respect herself? Squaring her shoulders, she looked at Joss and met his stare. Her heart pounded, but she refused to lower her gaze again.

"I want to help, but I can't if I don't know what's wrong." Joss's gentle voice, combined with the lines worrying his forehead, were nearly her undoing. She sniffled again but blinked fast, keeping the fresh tears at bay.

She wiped the dampness from her cheeks with the back of her hand and pushed herself away from the wall. The movement closed the distance between them until only a few inches separated them. She took a steadying breath. "I'm okay," she finally said in little more than a whisper, her voice hoarse from lack of use.

How long had it been since she'd spoken? Weeks? Months? Karak, the male the Alpha had given her to, hadn't liked for her to speak—or make any noise for that matter. Any time she'd pleaded with him for her freedom, she'd received a beating for her efforts.

Joss drew a sharp breath and his frown disappeared. He didn't quite smile, but pleasure shone in his eyes, and she was glad she'd said the words.

He opened his mouth, but a sound just outside the bedroom door stopped him short. An instant later, one of the biggest males she'd ever seen filled the frame. Although she'd caught a glimpse of him before and knew him to be part of the Komoro pack, she'd never met him. Violet took a small step, obstructing herself from his view with Joss standing between them.

"I knocked, but no one answered," the male said. He looked from Joss to her and back again, and to her amazement, his cheeks reddened. "I probably should have come back later."

"Khet, have you met my mate, Violet?" Joss asked the man.

"Not officially. Nice to meet you, Violet." The man didn't come into the room.

Crap. Was she expected to speak? Should she keep her mouth shut? She didn't know the rules here. She brought her hand up and clutched the back of Joss's shirt.

"Violet was about to go have a hot bath. If you don't mind waiting in the living room, I'll be right out," he said without missing a beat.

Khet gave her a small nod, then turned and left.

"I know you don't like being outside the room, but I think it's important you start getting used to your new surroundings. You're safe here." He sounded like a broken record saying it, but until she believed him, he'd keep repeating it.

She almost opened her mouth to protest, but each time she'd snuck out of the room to use the bathroom, she'd eyed the tub and had longed to use it. Freshening up at the sink wasn't nearly enough to make her feel clean. "I'd like that, thank you," she said before she lost her nerve.

The instant her words left her mouth, Joss's lips curled up into the most stunning smile she'd ever seen. Her heart did a little flip that had nothing to do with fear and everything to do with pleasing the man who'd been taking care of her so sweetly.

He glanced at her, and a little spark of humor danced in his eyes. "If you want me to get the bath ready, you'll have to let me go. Though I'll admit, I'd stand here with you all day if it's what you want."

She unfurled her fingers from his shirt, releasing him, more than a little surprised that she'd unconsciously hung on to him for so long. "Sorry, I shouldn't have done that."

"Don't be. And yes, you should have. I'm your mate. I will always protect you, Violet." He took the hand she'd dropped to her side, brought it to his lips, and gave her a chaste kiss on her knuckles. "Now, let's see about that bath."

# « CHAPTER 3 »

Joss couldn't contain his smile as he made his way to the living room. Not only had Violet spoken to him, but she'd turned to him for protection. Okay, so the reflexive action wasn't a huge declaration of undying trust and devotion, but it was a start, and it was a whole lot more than he'd expected so soon.

His smile, however, died on his lips the instant he caught a glimpse of Khet's furrowed brows and deep scowl. "What's going on?" he asked without preamble. It was no wonder Violet had been scared with Khet there. The man was huge. All the Erritrol wolves—the newest members of their pack—were. The fact that they were loyal and kind wouldn't even occur to someone who had suffered the abuse Violet had.

But Joss knew better. The man and the others were big, but they wouldn't harm a single one of their pack mates. Their size and power were what had prompted Delana to seek them out for protection in the first place.

Khet glanced down the hallway before addressing him. "Rennan spotted wolves hanging around the edges of our territory during his morning patrols. The Mahehkan scent is all along our forest's edges."

Every muscle in his body tightened. "Who's going after them? Has the team been dispatched yet?"

"No one. Argram has decided to wait and see what they'll do. He wants to re-establish the village once he's sure all of Roger's bastards are gone for good, and there's no way to know if those hanging around are Roger's men or some of the innocents that scattered when we attacked."

"I don't like it. Why not come to the village and speak with Argram? Why skulk around?"

Khet grunted something in his native tongue, then nodded. "That's why we've increased patrols."

"What do you need me to do?" He didn't want to leave Violet and risk losing that fragile bond they were forming, but to keep her safe, he would. He'd do anything.

"Nothing. You're to stay here for now. The unmated males are already out there. Argram just wants everyone in the village to be vigilant if they decide to go into the woods. He's not forbidding it, but be aware of what—and who's—around you."

As always, Argram's plan was sound. Their Alpha was not only fair, but he was smart and strategic. If he didn't want to make a move yet, Joss would respect that decision. "Fine. What about the bastard who hurt Violet? Any news there?"

A muscle ticked in Khet's jaw. "James hasn't identified Karak as one of the dead."

"Damn it." He'd hoped the man had died a slow and painful death. Knowing he still walked the earth after the things he'd put Violet through had fury ripping through every part of him. His wolf bristled, and it was all he could do to keep his growl from rumbling out.

"Rennan's out there tracking. It's only a matter of time before he catches the scents of those who escaped. They'll have to hunt sooner or later, and when they do, no amount of running will save them."

"Delana sent the things you requested. She would have brought them herself, but she's helping Amalija and Miga organize a welcome get-together for the new pack mates." He pointed to the bags he'd left by the door.

"Thanks. I appreciate it. I don't think we'll be going out in public for a while. Violet has barely eaten or come out of the room yet."

"Those bastards tried hard, but they didn't break the other women, and they won't have broken Violet, either. She'll be fine. She needs time."

"I swear, if I catch Karak anywhere near this village, I'll tear him apart myself."

Violet's scent wafted to him as he spoke the last words. If the sweetness filling his senses hadn't alerted him to her presence, her soft gasp would have.

He turned to find her in the doorway, one hand resting protectively on her belly, the other clenched at her side. "He's not dead?" she asked with a trembling voice.

Joss wouldn't lie. Not to her. Not about this—or anything else for that matter. "No, he didn't die in the battle. We'll find him, though. I promise you that."

She glanced at Khet, who stepped over to retrieve the bags from the floor. Her eyes widened, but she didn't back away.

"Delana says she'll come see you later today or maybe tomorrow. She picked out a few things for you. If there's anything in there you don't like, set it aside, and she'll return it." Khet handed the bags to Joss, but he kept his gaze on Violet.

"T-thank you."

Violet's fingers trembled when she lifted them from her belly, and her breaths came in quick, short pants. He was proud of her for having the courage to come out, but anyone could see the panic rising on her pale face.

"Did Lanie tell you when they're planning the get-together?" Joss asked, taking the attention from her and onto him again. Khet's eyes narrowed, but he didn't bother commenting on his use of the nickname. Joss had called his sister that since they'd been kids, and if his brother-in-law didn't like it, then he'd have to get used to it.

"Day after next, I think. You'd better confirm that with Delana, though," Khet said as he headed for the door.

"Thanks again for bringing that stuff over. I would never have known what to buy on my own."

Khet nodded and glanced over at Violet, giving her one of his rare smiles. "Was nice finally meeting you, Violet."

She swallowed hard. "Likewise."

Joss expected Violet to retreat to the bedroom as soon as Khet left, but she stood there, staring at him. Her breaths had slowed, and she didn't look as scared, but she remained silent.

"You look like you have something to say."

She swallowed and gave her head a little shake, then huffed and clenched her hands at her sides. "I have no money to pay you back for those things," she finally blurted out, her cheeks turning a deep rosy color.

It took a moment for what she'd said to register in his mind. He wasn't sure if he should laugh or pull at his hair. What the hell was she talking about? "You're my mate, Violet. It's my honor and my pleasure to provide you with everything you need. The food in the kitchen? It's yours. If you're hungry, help yourself. You're free to read the books on the shelves, and if you don't find any that you like, we can get you something you would enjoy reading more. Even those T-shirts in the top drawer you seem fond of, you're free to take them. Wear them. Do whatever. I don't mind."

"How did you—"

"I can smell you on the fabric," he supplied as he smiled and stepped closer. "Before you get upset…it makes me happy to have your scent on them—on me—when I'm wearing them."

She opened her mouth to speak, but then shut it, pulling her bottom lip between her teeth in a way that made him want to have a taste. "Come on, let's see what Delana chose for you," he said before he could make good on his desire to kiss her.

# « CHAPTER 4 »

Violet had learned to be afraid of gifts—or rather, gift-givers. It hadn't taken her long after Roger had taken over as Alpha of the old Mahehkan pack to figure out that the price of kindness was sometimes much greater than the cost of a present. But one look at Joss, with his eagerness to please shining brightly in his eyes, had her heart fluttering for a reason so far apart from fear that she could hardly recognize it anymore.

Hope. Did she dare let her guard down with this man? Delana, his sister, had been gentle and kind. But more importantly, she was...free. She came and went as she pleased, moving about the village at will. As far as Violet could see, the woman was unharmed. She seemed happy—deliriously happy. When she spoke of her mate, she positively glowed.

With more determination than bravery, Violet crossed over to Joss and held her hand out, taking one of the overflowing bags from him. When her fingers came up steady—more or less—her confidence rose. "Thank you."

"You're welcome. And when you're feeling up to it, you can go pick things for yourself."

The baby chose that moment to give her a good kick to the ribs on her right. She gasped and clutched her belly. The instant she did, Joss's smile dropped.

"What's wrong?" he asked in a rush.

If ever there was a man who was unsure about a pregnant woman, Joss was him. "The baby is active today. He's a strong kicker."

His eyes rounded and he frowned. "Does it hurt? I'm not sure if I like that."

She almost smiled at the seriousness in his gaze. What did he think he'd be able to do about it if it did? "It doesn't. Not at all. I'm glad he's moving around more today. I think he appreciates the meal." Heat rushed to her cheeks, but she didn't look away. She'd eaten as well as she could throughout her pregnancy. She wouldn't feel bad for things that were beyond her control.

Joss's gaze flew back to hers from where he'd been looking at her belly. "You know it's a he?"

Try as she might, there was no stopping the smile from emerging at that point. The goofy look on Joss's face wouldn't allow it. "I don't, actually, but it's better than calling him or her an it."

He nodded gravely. "You're right. I'm sure the baby wouldn't appreciate that."

The small burst of joy deep inside her dimmed a little. Joss would make a great father. If things were different, she could see herself building a future—a family—with him.

Damn Karak for taking yet another thing from her. Even now, when he was nowhere near the Komoro village, he was controlling her future. The question was...would she allow it? She yearned for a normal life, for a doting mate and loving father for her child. Why shouldn't she have those things? The ache in her heart grew, stealing her breath. As much as she wanted it, taking on raising another man's child was too much to ask, even of a good man like Joss.

"Hey, whatever you're thinking, stop. Put it out of your head. I much prefer that sweet smile you had on moments ago to the frown you've got now." He lifted his hand to brush her hair behind her ear. He caught the stray lock between his thumb and finger, letting it slip out of his grasp.

The moment lengthened into an awkward silence.

"Listen, I know you're still tired. Why don't you show me what Delana bought later? I have to check on the progress at a new build in the village. I'll be back soon." Joss dropped his hand again. "You can lock the door behind me if you want."

Her heart stuttered, then raced ahead at full speed. He was leaving? She swallowed hard and gave him a quick nod, even though the voice inside her screamed for him to stay. As far as she knew, he hadn't left her unprotected since he'd brought her here. What if others were close? What if they weren't as honorable? Heart still pounding, she tried to keep the panic at bay. She'd be fine. She wasn't in the ramshackle shack anymore. She wasn't a prisoner. "I think I'll go lie down now," she told him. If she didn't get this under control, her legs wouldn't hold her for much longer.

"Violet," his deep, steady voice stopped her before she could flee. "Would you like to come with me? I can wait until you've rested."

It was on the tip of her tongue to say no. She should learn to depend on herself and no one else, but when she opened her mouth, the words "Yes, please, if it's not too much trouble," slipped out.

She wasn't sure what to expect, but if anything, Joss looked even happier with her request. "It's no trouble at all. Have your nap. I'll be here when you wake."

Taking the second bag from his hands, she gave him a small smile, as wobbly as it was, and headed back toward the bedroom. When she glanced at him over her shoulder before going in, he was grinning from ear to ear.

Her legs still shook, and she was probably crazy for even trusting this man at all, but she was determined to make a life for herself and her baby. She'd have to wait and see if that life would include Joss, but she owed it to her child to come out of her past intact and whole, either way. And that meant pushing past her fears and learning to live again.

## « CHAPTER 5 »

Joss couldn't believe the strides Violet had made in the past couple of hours. As if hearing her sweet voice hadn't been enough, she'd come to him in the living room, held a conversation, and agreed to an outing.

Nothing could wipe the smile from his face. He stood at the bedroom door, listening for any sign of movement on the other side, but all was quiet. Violet had looked exhausted. Rather than sit around and wait, he figured he'd get to some jobs he'd been putting off. When they moved to the new house, he wanted to leave this one in tip-top shape for the new resident. There were many new wolves in the pack, and they'd need a roof over their heads. And as hard as the men worked, they wouldn't all have new homes before winter hit. Many would have to share homes until spring, but not him and Violet. As soon as he'd found her, he'd known a new house was in order. They needed the extra space for the baby.

Sure, they could make do with this one for a while, but he had more than enough credits for the new one, and someone else would benefit from him vacating this one. It was a win-win situation.

The loose shutter on the front window needed to be secured, and a couple of the back steps needed replacing, but those would have to wait a while longer. Joss didn't want to disturb Violet's sleep with his hammering. That only left painting for outside work, and the day was too beautiful to stay indoors.

The front porch was first on the list. Pulling the supplies he'd need from the tool shed, Joss set off to work, but not before opening the front door, leaving only the screen door closed so that he could hear Violet if she should awaken before he finished.

Even though it was autumn and the breeze was cool, with the sun beating on his back, it didn't take long for beads of sweat to trickle down his spine. He pulled his T-shirt off and draped it over the far railing where he could grab it before heading in the back door. After more than an hour of steady work, the porch looked as good as new. Another few minutes and he could call it a day. Violet would be waking soon and they could go to their new home. Of course, she had no idea the build they would be seeing was to be hers, but she was doing so well with everything, that he considered telling her about it when they were on site. He'd need her input to make sure it was to her liking anyway.

"Looking good, Joss," Delana called from the sidewalk.

He brushed the last stroke of paint onto the last step and put the brush down, admiring his handiwork for a second before joining his sister. "Thanks. I imagine one or two of the women will take this place over once we move out. I want it to be ready for them."

"Good idea. I know a couple of the men have bunked together and are making room for the others, too."

"Are you coming in?"

"I really can't, but I'll pop by tomorrow for sure. Khet tells me he's met Violet." Delana bounced on the balls of her feet, her excitement bubbling from her entire body.

Joss couldn't help grinning back. "Yeah. She's doing great today. Better than I expected. We're going to walk up to the new house when she wakes from her nap."

Before Lanie could say anything more, the screen door flew open and Violet rushed out, bare feet landing on the fresh, white paint. Eyes wide and body rigid, she looked like the devil himself was after her—until her eyes fell upon him.

"Shit." He dashed across the yard, not bothering to say good-bye to his sister. The last thing Violet needed was to get a splinter in her foot from a rough board, or—heaven forbid—step on a nail. Not that there were any as far as he knew, but he wasn't taking any chances.

When he started across the yard, her hands flew up to cover her mouth and with a strangled cry, she bolted back into the house. *Damn it.* He'd meant to make sure she was okay, not scare the living daylights out of her.

Heedless of the wet paint, Joss sprinted after her. Even if he hadn't known she'd go into the master bedroom, he would have been able to follow each dainty, white footstep on the dark hardwood floors.

He was tracking more of his own with every one of his long strides, but toeing off his shoes would have wasted too much time. He found her sitting on the bed. Her whole body was shaking, and he could have kicked himself for doing that to her.

"I-I thought you were gone," she said in a rush when he stopped in front of her.

Joss looked at her for a second then groaned. "And you got scared."

Her bottom lip wobbled and she wrung her hands in her lap. "I didn't mean to step in the paint. I'm s-sorry."

"Before we get into any of that, are you okay?" he asked her, crouching in front of her so that he was at her eye level.

"I'm okay."

"Good. That's all that matters."

"But I tracked paint all over the house."

He glanced at the floor behind him. "So did I. I'll touch up the paint and clean up the mess. No harm done," Joss assured her.

It took a moment, but eventually, her shoulders relaxed and the fear shining in her eyes subsided.

"We do have a little problem, though," he told her softly, not wanting to frighten her again. Her gaze followed his down to her feet. "I know this isn't going to be easy for you, but I'd like to carry you to the bathroom so we can wash your feet. If you don't want that, you can walk. I won't be angry. I'll just clean up more footprints. Understood?"

She blinked her big brown eyes up at him a few times. He could almost see the gears in her head working, but he kept his mouth shut, giving her the time she needed to make up her mind.

"Okay."

"Okay?" His heart skipped a beat at the thought of holding her in his arms, if only for the few seconds it would take him to get her to the bathroom.

## « CHAPTER 6 »

One of the most vivid nightmares Violet had had since her rescue had woken her from her nap. When she'd come out of the room to find Joss gone, the panic she'd shoved aside earlier had reared its ugly head, and she'd rushed out of the house to find him. The relief that had flooded her when she saw him standing at the end of the yard, speaking with Delana, died a quick death when she realized what she had done.

The wet, sticky paint on the soles of her feet registered as Joss started running toward her. She hadn't thought. She'd just run. Her fight or flight instinct was strong, and it almost always chose flight. Her horror had exploded when she'd realized she'd made matters worse by decorating his lovely floors with her painted footprints. Yet he sat there on his heels, concern shining in his eyes, asking her if she was okay. He should have been livid, yet he didn't seem angry in the least. He'd even said he wasn't.

Joss wasn't Karak. It was time she stopped treating him as though he was.

"Yes, you can carry me," she said over the pounding of her heart. Deep inside, she knew Joss wouldn't hurt her, but that fear was hard to shake when she'd been beaten for much smaller offenses almost daily for the past three years.

He reached down and untied his shoes before standing and kicking them off, not even looking to see where they landed with their wet-painted heels. "I'm going to put one arm under your knees and the other behind your back. Hang on to me if you want, but I won't drop you even if you don't."

Drop her? The thought hadn't even crossed her mind. She'd known all along that he was no weakling, but with his shirt off, the proof was right there in front of her. Hard muscle carved his chest and abdomen and made his arms bulge in just the right way, making her feel small and dainty.

Joss moved slowly, letting her adjust to his nearness. When he lifted her from the bed and pulled her up against his chest, she held her breath. Leaving her arms down felt awkward, so she slid them up around his neck.

"Still doing okay?" he asked her, his minty breath fanning against her cheek. For a split second, she was tempted to turn her face and brush her lips against his.

She ducked her head so that he couldn't see her face or the ridiculous blush that had to be staining her cheeks. "Yes, I'm okay."

He turned slowly and took her out of the room. She'd swear Joss sniffed her hair before a soft moan reached her ear.

"I'll set you down on the edge of the tub. We'll have you all cleaned up in no time," Joss told her as he put her down.

Joss's voice had taken a huskier tone while he'd carried her, and something stirred. Not something—someone. The she-wolf buried deep inside her lifted her head, as though taking notice of her surroundings for the first time. She hadn't roused for much of anything in months. It had been too busy trying to protect her and the baby—and simply surviving—to do much of anything else.

She followed Joss's movements as he turned from her and set the water in the tub for her for the second time that day, adjusting it until the temperature was perfect before straightening. He reached into the cabinet, pulling out a washcloth, and then took the soap from the holder.

When he turned to face her again, she had to tear her gaze away from the rippling muscle display. He wasn't trying to impress her by flexing and showing off, but he didn't have to. She wasn't blind. She noticed how well put-together he was. With his shirt off and his jeans hanging low on his hips, he was a sight to behold. If she didn't stop staring, she'd be wiping the drool off her chin and giving him ideas she had no business giving him.

Bringing her gaze to his, she found him smiling at her. *Damn, he's gorgeous.* His eyebrows rose, and he looked at her expectantly. When she kept staring up at him, his smile widened.

What had she missed?

"I guess you didn't hear me," he finally said. "Would you mind lifting your foot for me?"

Crap. Yeah, she'd been too busy ogling and hadn't been paying attention. "Sorry." She did as he asked, and he took hold of her ankle.

"It's okay. I don't know if soap will get rid of it all, but we can't risk using a stronger chemical on your skin in case it affects the baby."

Joss shifted his position, getting down on his knees at the edge of the tub before giving the sole of her foot the first gentle swipe. He took his time, getting between each of her toes even though she was sure none of the paint had made its way in there, but it felt too good to stop him. When he stroked the soft cloth over her insole, she couldn't keep the moan from slipping past her lips.

He glanced at her and grinned. "I think you deserve a foot massage."

Before she could protest, he dropped the cloth and had both hands wrapped around her freshly cleaned foot. His thumbs pressed into the soft tissue, kneading and rubbing in a way designed to make her melt. Okay, up until a few minutes ago, she would have sworn his sculpted chest was his best physical asset, but his hands were definitely in contention for the title. She tried to keep her moans to herself, but each time one got away from her, his grin came back.

"That's one," he finally said when she was a puddle sitting on the edge of the tub. He set her foot down and took the facecloth, rinsed, and lathered it again, then held his hand out for her.

She didn't hesitate, lifting her other foot for him. "Where did you learn to do that?" she asked him. Did he make it a habit of massaging women's feet? A spark of something that felt way too much like jealousy blossomed in her chest.

Joss shrugged, making the muscles in his shoulder bunch, drawing her gaze. "I guess I'm doing it right, then? It's not something I've ever done."

"I never would have guessed. It feels wonderful. Thank you."

He smiled at her again and went to work on her other foot. Neither spoke as he cleaned, then massaged her foot. The tension in her body fell away under his ministrations, leaving her more relaxed than she had been in months, maybe even years. If his hands did that to her with a foot rub, she couldn't imagine what kind of magic would happen if he set his sights on massaging her whole body.

The thought of his hands on her back, her legs, and her chest had her body tensing again, but not in nervousness or fear. A fresh wave of awareness flooded her as he stood and reached for a soft towel. Her nipples tightened beneath her shirt, and she was glad he was focused on her feet once more. She had to get those ideas out of her head. Nothing good would come of thinking of him like that. She was pregnant, for crying out loud, and not just a little. If her calculations were right, she had a little over two months to go. There was no way he'd want to do anything remotely sexual with her.

"There, that should do it," he said, his voice a little strained. "If you want to wear one of your new outfits, I'll wait for you in the living room."

Before she could say anything, he spun on his heels and was out the door.

## « CHAPTER 7 »

Joss waited until he heard the bedroom door close behind Violet before leaning against the wall, closing his eyes and moaning. Having her in his arms, touching her body, being enveloped her scent, had been an exercise of the sweetest kind of torture. But when she'd relaxed and her sweet sighs had drifted to his ears, it had taken all his strength to continue and not reveal how much her nearness had been affecting him.

The sounds of her pleasure had brought images of them together to the forefront of his mind. Of him pleasing her in other ways. Her body, naked and on display, willing and waiting for him to taste every inch of her. Blood had rushed to his cock, and he'd been thankful he'd crouched down so she hadn't been able to see the evidence through his jeans. Even now he throbbed so hard he could hardly think. He had to do something. Otherwise, his current state would not dissipate by the time she came out, and the last thing she needed was to see him like this.

With a groan, he pushed away from the wall and headed into the kitchen. He'd get rid of the footprints on the floor. Maybe by the time he finished, he'd be able to stand upright without embarrassing himself—or worse, scaring Violet.

He was two-thirds of the way done by the time she came out. His breath caught in his throat when he looked up at her. She'd changed into a new outfit. The white shirt hugged her curves, yet left room for her growing belly. Her breasts were on display beneath the soft material, but not in an overtly sexual way, which made him want to moan. The innocent look was as sexy as anything he'd ever seen. The jeans she had on hugged her body, and he had to wonder how comfortable that would be and if it was good for the baby.

Violet nibbled on her lip and lifted the hem of her shirt, obviously reading his question in his eyes. "It has a panel at the front," she supplied.

Huh. Funny, Joss had been around pregnant women before, but he'd never felt the need to question what they wore. With Violet, everything was different. He had to make sure she was comfortable and safe. Always. "That's good. Are they comfy? You look fantastic, by the way," he finally said when he found his voice.

She nodded and smiled. "Very. Thanks again."

"Let me get this done, and then we can go. Did you want a snack first? There's plenty of food in the fridge," he offered.

She glanced toward the kitchen but didn't make a move to go.

"It would make me really happy if you helped yourself, Violet, but that's not important. Take what you need for you and for the baby. You've gone without for way too long. It's time you put that behind you. Go ahead. I'll only be a few minutes."

Violet stepped toward the kitchen but then stopped. "Would you like me to fix something for you?" she asked, her voice soft—uncertain.

The woman was absolutely perfect. If Joss thought Violet would accept it, he'd go over and give her a tight hug and maybe a kiss, but he wasn't an idiot. It was way too soon for anything like that. "Sure. Whatever you're having will be fine."

Her small smile and quick nod were enough to fill him with joy all over again, not that it had gone very far to start. What he had done in his past to deserve such an amazing woman, he had no idea, but he was grateful for it.

He scrubbed the few remaining footprints with quick, efficient wipes until no trace of the incident remained. He'd deal with fixing the paint job outside later.

When he entered the kitchen, he found Violet sitting at the table with a plate in front of her and another waiting for him. She'd prepared meat sandwiches and had a glass of juice sitting next to each one. "Go ahead and start. I'll wash my hands."

"I can wait. It's the least I can do after you cleaned up my mess." She sipped her juice, fingers as steady as could be.

"It was nothing." He took his seat, pleased when his knee brushed against hers under the table and she made no move to pull it away. He took a huge bite of his sandwich. This was the first meal his mate had ever prepared for him, and he'd savor every bite.

She'd taken her own in her hand but watched as he chewed and swallowed.

"Delicious. Thanks for making it," he told her once his mouth was empty. She rewarded him with her smile.

"You're welcome."

They ate the rest of their meal in a silence more comfortable than he'd imagined they would share for a long time, cementing one thing in his mind. His mate had been through more than any woman should ever have to go through, but she was strong and resilient. She was going to be fine.

*** 

Other than when she'd been carried to the Komoro village, which she hardly remembered due to the condition she'd been in, Violet hadn't been out in months. She'd been a prisoner. The sounds and smells of the village were unlike anything from her recent past, but they did bring her back to a brighter time. Back before Roger and his asshole thugs took the home she once shared with her parents and destroyed it, killing them and capturing her.

The Komoro people walked around, chatting, happy—free. Women were unaccompanied. Most of them glanced in her direction as she and Joss walked past, but their curiosity was nothing more than polite interest. She got smiles from everyone to the point where she was a little overwhelmed by all the unintended attention. She found herself walking closer to Joss, her shoulder brushing against his arm now and then. She tried stopping, but each time she did, she ended up right next to him.

Joss pointed out the small shops along the main street. "Anytime you want to get anything, tell them to use my credits. I have more than enough. No one will question it."

She should protest, but it would do no good, so she nodded. Maybe she could find a way to earn some before the baby arrived. He would need clothes and other things.

"Joss," a deep, very male voice boomed from somewhere close.

Violet tensed and pressed herself against him. In an instant, he lifted his arm and pulled her to his left side, sheltering her.

"Argram. Nice to see you," Joss said as he held his hand out. "I'd like to introduce my mate, Violet. We would have been by to see you sooner, but Violet has been a little under the weather."

"Understandable," the huge man said.

"Violet, this is our Alpha, Argram."

"P-pleased to meet you, Alpha," she stammered.

"Same." The Alpha looked at her, then at Joss. The men exchanged a funny look, but then, before either spoke, a tall, stunningly beautiful woman came around the corner with an adorable little toddler in her arms, and the Alpha's face softened. "And here is my mate. Miga, this is Violet, Joss's mate."

Miga took one look at her and smiled. It wasn't a polite, getting-through-introductions kind of smile, but a genuine show of joy that Violet couldn't help but respond to. "I've heard a lot about you, but since I hadn't seen you around, I was beginning to think you weren't real. Nice to meet you, Violet. This little terror is Malec," she said, bouncing her little boy on her hip, making his hair flop up and down on his head.

The little guy giggled at his mother's antics. "Again," he demanded when she stopped.

"Nice to meet all of you," she said. Argram was intimidating as hell, but Miga gave off a friendly vibe.

"When are you due?" the other woman asked.

Her hand automatically came up to her belly. "I'm not sure. I think maybe another couple of months. I had no way of keeping track." She wished she could have done better for her unborn child, but the truth was, surviving was the only thing she could do most days.

"Oh, so you're having a Christmas baby." Miga's smile widened further. "Remember the stories about the man in the red suit, Argram? Santa Claus? That celebration is coming up in a couple of months. Maybe the baby will be born at Christmas. Wouldn't that be wonderful?"

The Alpha looked at his mate with a lost look on his face. "That would be something."

Miga rolled her eyes at her mate. "Yes, it would be. Listen, Violet, we're organizing a get-together for all the new members of the pack. It's happening in two days. We'd love for you to come. You don't have to do anything, just come meet the rest of the pack and have a bit of fun."

"I-I don't know." She looked at Joss, hoping he'd rescue her.

"I think it's a great idea. If you want to go, we will. Maybe we can wait and see if you're feeling up to it when the time comes," Joss suggested.

Leave it to him to give her an out. At least if she didn't show up, she wouldn't look like she was trying to avoid everyone.

Miga handed Malec to her mate, then took his free hand. "Great. Well, I have tons of things to organize, and this little guy needs a nap in the worst way, but we'll see each other again soon."

"They seem nice," Violet said once they were walking again and out of the Alpha couple's earshot.

"They are. Argram is intense, but he's fair. And don't let Miga fool you. She's got a heart of gold, but she's fierce in her own right. She's the Alpha's perfect complement."

"I'll be sure to remember that."

The sounds of construction reached her ears before they rounded the next corner. The lot was bigger than the ones on either side of it, and it looked like the house would be larger, as well. Violet was a little shocked to see both men and women working together to get the job done.

"What do you think?" Joss asked, his voice holding all the excitement of a child at Christmas.

She looked around as he took her hand and pulled her onto the property. "It looks like it's going to be a house."

He gave her an odd look. "It is. It's going to be *your* house, Violet."

"What? I don't understand." She didn't want a house. As silly as it seemed, she thought she would stay with Joss. What if Karak came into the village? Or one of the Komoro men showed up at her door? The ever-present panic she'd shoved aside exploded through her, making her whole body shake. Of course, he'd want her to have her own place. She was carrying Karak's child. He wouldn't want to deal with that on a daily basis.

His brows furrowed and he took her hands in his. "I'm having it built for you—for us." Joss's smile dropped. "I know some of the others will be returning to the old Mahehkan village once it's safe to do so, but I'd hoped you might decide to stay here. With me. If you don't like it, we can live in the house we have now until the spring."

She blinked fast as his words registered in her mind. He wasn't trying to get rid of her. "But, the baby..."

Joss stroked his thumb over her knuckles. "The baby will have a mother and father who love and adore him—or her." The uncertainty in his eyes was almost her undoing. She wanted that. Wanted him. How can one man seem so wonderful? He couldn't be that perfect—could he?

With a smile that was more wobbly than sure, she gave him a little nod. There was still a long way for them to go, and they had to get to know one another, but maybe things would be okay.

Joss's face lit up, and with a loud whoop, he gathered her into his arms and spun her around. By the time he set her on her feet, she was giggling and had all but forgotten where they were.

"Come on, let's check out what they've done. The men are working on the nursery today."

# « CHAPTER 8 »

Violet sat on the couch, waiting for Joss to come back. She'd bounced back and forth between staying home alone and going with him many times all morning. Eventually, her desire to look good for the welcome party later in the day had won out. For the first few minutes after he'd left, she'd half expected her heart to pound right out of her chest. But she'd forced herself to stay behind—barely. After many deep breaths—and one hyperventilating incident—she'd calmed enough to leave the front door. If she wanted any kind of normalcy in her life, she would have to push past her fears. Besides, if she was going to have to meet a bunch of new people today, she wanted to look her best—at least, as good as a seven-plus months pregnant woman could.

There wasn't much she could do with her long, straight hair, but it was clean, and the shampoo Joss had bought for her made it shine and smell nice. She dusted her cheeks with blush and put a bit of liner and mascara on, making her pale face look a little less white. Then with a simple gloss over her lips, she looked presentable. She'd have to remember to thank Delana for being so thoughtful. As kind and generous as Joss was, she seriously doubted he was responsible for those items she'd found in one of the bags.

She stood and paced to the door, not because she was overly nervous, but because she liked the way the pretty pink dress she had on flowed around her thighs. She'd never had much of a wardrobe before Roger had taken over, but after, she'd had none. They'd barely kept her clothed at all.

Her heart skipped a beat when she spotted him walking down the street, a smile playing on his lips. There was a quiet strength about him, one that she—and her wolf—couldn't help responding to. One that he didn't outwardly show but was evident in his every action. His patience and gentle care, more than anything else, were what had gotten her through her first week since the rescue. They gave her the courage to try to reclaim a life she hadn't expected she would have the opportunity to live.

A flicker of shame grew in her chest. In the weeks before her rescue, she'd resigned herself to her fate. It wasn't that she'd stopped caring about what happened, but each beating and every foul touch had vanquished all hope. She'd even prayed that she'd find the strength to resist Karak one more time, maybe say something or even spit on the bastard. She knew she'd never escape, but she hoped to provoke him so that he'd go that little extra step further and end her existence. She hadn't found that strength. As much as she'd wanted it to end, a small part of her had refused to allow it.

When Joss looked up and found her waiting for him on the other side of the screen door, his smile lit his entire face. Her breath caught and after a moment, she smiled back. She wasn't that prisoner in that dingy, little shack anymore. Deep in her soul, she knew that she wasn't responsible for Karak's actions. She was taking her life back. Those bastards weren't going to win.

Before Joss could reach the door, she pushed it open for him. She should have backed up to let him through, but she stayed where she was, partially blocking the doorway.

He looked at her—from the top of her head all the way down to the flat shoes she'd put on, and then back up again to meet her gaze. "You look amazing, Violet," he said when he reached her.

"Thank you."

Joss's gaze flicked to her lips and he licked his own, but when he leaned in, he gave her a soft peck on the cheek before slipping past her.

"How did things go while I was gone?"

She hadn't told him she'd been scared to be alone. She hadn't needed to. Her reactions were obvious to anyone, and Joss was extra observant, never missing a thing. At least, not that she could see.

"Better than I thought it would. I was nervous at first, but then I did okay."

He reached out and stroked her cheek, leaving her skin tingling. "Be proud of all you've overcome in such a short time. You're doing great. Don't forget that."

When he brought his hand down to his side again, she missed the touch, but she smiled and nodded. Her heart soared at his praise, the words warming her to the depths of her soul. Maybe she shouldn't care what others thought of her, but she did, and Joss especially. He was different. Pleasing him wasn't about survival or lessening a punishment. It was about doing something that felt *right*. For her.

"Did you have something to eat while I was gone? I don't know what time they'll be serving the meal at the party. I'd hate for you to go hungry in the meantime."

"I did. I'm good to go." It wasn't that she'd been horribly hungry, but once she'd showered and gotten ready, she hadn't been able to resist the preserves and fresh bread he always seemed to have on hand. It wasn't the most nutritious snack, but what it lacked in nutrients, it made up for in sticky yumminess.

His smile lit his face again. "Good. I'm going to freshen up. Then we can go."

Violet didn't move from her spot until he had closed the bathroom door and the sound of the shower running reached her ears. Joss was hers for the taking. She just had to be brave enough to do it.

# « CHAPTER 9 »

The pack house was almost full by the time Joss opened the door and ushered Violet inside. Tables had been set up along the outside walls for people to sit and talk, leaving the center open for groups to chat, and later, maybe even dance. The thought of taking Violet in his arms, even if only to spin her around the dance floor, was enough to send his heart racing a little.

Although strained, her smile stayed in place as they made their way inside. Damn, she was beautiful. The pink dress she had on hugged her breasts in a demure, yet sexy way, while the skirt flared around her belly, hips, and thighs, ending above the knee. Stunning. He could happily sit there and look at her all day and night and never tire of it.

Soft music played in the background. Later, they would turn it up, but for now, it was an unobtrusive background noise, giving the gathering a cozy feel. A few of the new pack members sat together, looking more like they were ready to flee than to have a good time, but at least they were there. Joss had to respect them for their bravery alone.

"Would you like something to drink? I'm sure they have a fruit punch over there somewhere," he pointed to a long table on the other side of the room.

"Yes, please."

Violet's strained voice had him focusing his attention on her again. "Doing okay? Do we need to leave?" As much as he appreciated all the effort the women had gone through to organize the event, he'd whisk Violet out of there in a heartbeat if it was too much for her to handle.

Taking a deep breath, she shook her head. "I'm okay. We can stay."

"You're sure?"

The small smile she gave him lost some of its tightness, and his own melted away. "Would you like a drink?"

"Is it okay if I go with you?"

"Absolutely," he assured her. In fact, he would have been shocked if she had stayed behind. He was completely at ease in the pack's presence, but she wasn't. Not yet, anyway.

Drinks in hand, he found a spot where their backs would be to a wall, ensuring that she didn't have to worry about anyone coming up behind her. Already the crowd thickened as more people arrived. The last time so many were present at a gathering had been when Argram had been named Alpha in his place. A small part of him regretted not having taken the position when it had been available, but it was minute, and each time he saw Argram in action, he knew the Alpha was the right man for the job. He wasn't a beta by any stretch of the imagination, but he wasn't a natural leader—never had been. He didn't wish for the responsibility of the entire pack. He'd been ready to assume the role if need be, but handing over the reins once Argram came along had been a no-brainer for him. And now the pack was thriving. It had been the right decision.

Delana was the first to stop and speak to them. She gave him a hug and Violet a warm smile. He could tell that she wanted to hug Violet, too, but she held herself back. He'd have to remember to thank her for it later. Right then, he wasn't sure Violet would be able to handle too much physical contact. Her grip on his fingers was cutting off the circulation to his fingertips as it was, but he sure as hell wasn't complaining. She hadn't let go, even when he'd poured their punch.

"Are you enjoying yourself so far?" Delana asked Violet.

"We just got here, but yeah, so far so good."

Her voice was steadier now. *That's my girl.*

"I haven't had the chance to thank you for getting all these clothes for me. And the makeup. Thank you," she continued without prompting.

Delana smiled. "It was my pleasure. I love shopping. Especially with my brother's money."

The women chatted for a few minutes as he looked over the crowd. Khet came in, followed by Argram, both men scowling deeper than usual. Argram met his gaze and indicated the door with a quick glance, wordlessly asking him to go outside.

Joss looked down at Violet, who was now laughing at something Delana had told her. He knew he couldn't take her away, and he sure as hell couldn't leave her there.

He gave the Alpha a small shake of the head, hoping he'd understand. As always, Argram assessed the situation and nodded back. Whatever they needed to talk about would wait. Joss let out the breath he'd been holding and turned his attention back to the women.

"M-maybe you and Khet could come over for dinner one day next week," Violet suggested. Her fingers gripped his even tighter.

When she looked at him, uncertainty shining brightly in her eyes, he smiled. "That's a wonderful idea."

"We'd love to," Delana said as her mate joined them.

"We'd love to...what?" Khet asked as he wrapped an arm around Delana's waist, pulling her right up against his side.

"Violet and Joss have invited us to their home for dinner next week," Delana supplied as she tipped her head up for Khet's kiss.

Violet watched the exchange between the two, not missing a thing. Some of the tension she'd still held on to melted away. She didn't release his hand, but her fingers loosened around his.

"Ah, yes, sounds great," Khet finally said when he looked at them again. "I'm patrolling Monday and Tuesday, but Wednesday could work."

Violet swallowed hard but then nodded. "As long as it's okay with Joss, we can do it on Wednesday."

So much was happening so fast, Joss could barely contain himself. Delana and Khet had said all the right things, setting his mate at ease, and then, without even missing a beat, finalized things so that she couldn't easily back out. They were pushing her out of her comfort zone while still letting her call the shots. Genius.

"Wednesday it is," he added.

"Delana, may I speak with you privately?" Khet asked.

Talk—*right*. Joss knew damned well that if Khet got Delana alone, talking was the last thing that would happen, and by the look on Delana's face, she knew it, too.

"Of course, love. We'll see you guys on Wednesday," Delana said as she slipped her hand into Khet's.

Once the couple left, the stream of people pausing to speak with them didn't seem to stop. As soon as one person or group left, another would walk on over. Most of them were the Komoro pack coming to welcome Violet, but a few of the women from the old Mahehkan pack came by, as well. Tears fell, and hugs were exchanged. It was like a sorority of survivors reuniting.

Joss stood with her, joining the conversation when needed, but for the most part, Violet was holding her own. She was caught up in another bear hug from one of the other women when the pack house door opened and a petite woman with long, straight black hair came in.

The woman looked around the room, holding her head high and her chin jutted in the air, almost daring anyone to cross her. As petite as she was, she looked like she could kick butt and take names. Her gaze drifted over the crowd, glancing over them only to continue a short distance away, but then, her head whipped back, and she looked right at him and Violet again.

Her eyes widened and her hands flew up to cover her mouth. In the next instant, she was moving toward them. By the time she got halfway through the room, she was running. Hearing the commotion, Violet pulled out of the other woman's arms and spotted the one running to them.

Violet's strangled cry filled the now overly silent room. He reached for her, intent on pulling her behind him, away from danger, but Violet wasn't there. She was rushing to meet the woman, catching her in her arms and holding her tight. Her soft sobs filled the silence.

Staring seemed intrusive, but there was no way he was leaving Violet or even moving without her knowing where he was in case she needed him. When the two finally disentangled themselves, Violet sought him, and he was glad he was where she'd left him. She gave him a wobbly smile and took the other woman's hand, pulling her toward him.

"Joss, this is my sister. Zeyde." Violet wiped away the dampness on her cheeks. "I-I thought she was dead. Karak told me she was. He lied."

Zeyde gave him an appraising look.

"I'm pleased to meet you, Zeyde," Joss said, extending his hand. Hugging her didn't seem right, and looking at her, he couldn't imagine she'd welcome it.

# « CHAPTER 10 »

Violet's heart had yet to slow. Seeing Zeyde for the first time in three years wasn't a surprise, it was a shock. The last time she'd seen her older sister, they had both been taken by Roger and his men. She shoved the horrible memories away. Eventually, she'd have to examine them to get past them fully, but not yet. She couldn't. With the baby on the way, she needed to focus on the good things in her life, not the horrors of her past.

After she'd introduced Zeyde and Joss, he'd led them to a table in one corner of the room where they could talk. He still hovered nearby, but he'd excused himself, giving her and her sister some time alone.

"Where have you been?" she asked.

Zeyde looked around, not missing a thing. She was different. Stronger. It wasn't just physical, either. She looked like she could—and would—take over the world if given any reason to.

"They kept me locked up for the first year. My body healed slowly. Once they started letting me out again, I looked for you, but you were gone. None of the women had seen you in months. I searched the village, but you'd disappeared. Roger claimed to have killed you himself."

Joss's growl rumbled from a few feet away, making her aware that although he wasn't with her, he was paying attention. She smiled at him, assuring him she was okay. He took a deep breath and unclenched his fists.

"What's with the bodyguard?" Zeyde asked.

"He's not a bodyguard. He's my mate."

"Your what?" Zeyde practically snarled.

"My mate. Joss is a good man, Zeyde."

"He's a man. That should be enough to make you stay away from him."

"Joss has been gentle and kind. I'm certain if you get to know him, you'll agree."

"I won't get to know him. I won't be staying. As soon as it's safe to go, I'm going back, and you're coming with me."

Violet couldn't believe the vehemence in her sister's words. "I'm staying. I don't ever want to go back there."

Zeyde looked at her and for a moment, the soft soul of her sister—the one she knew and loved—shone through. "Suit yourself, but don't say I didn't warn you when all these *gentlemen* turn out to be rabid, mangy dogs like the rest of them."

Her sister looked at Joss, not bothering to hide her loathing. "If you lay so much as a finger on my baby sister, it'll be the last thing you do. I'll make sure of it," she threatened before she stood.

"Where are you going?" Violet asked, standing with her sister as panic rushed to the surface. Zeyde was her only living relative.

"I'm staying with one of the women here in the village. The only reason I came in at all was that Reyelle caught sight of you and came to find me. I didn't believe it, but I had to see for myself."

"Will I see you again?" she asked, hoping that after all these years, she wouldn't lose her sister again so soon.

Zeyde's gaze, always roving the crowd, came back to rest on her. "Of course, you will. You're my sister. I won't stay, but that doesn't mean I won't come back from time to time. How else will I make sure *he* doesn't hurt you?" The words could have been a cute sisterly thing to say, but the way she said it with her voice raised and the emphasis on the *he*—it wasn't in jest.

"I'll be okay, I really will, but if that's the reason that will have you coming to visit, then I'm okay with that." She heard Joss snort and gave him a little wink. His eyes widened, as did his smile, so she grinned at him before turning her attention back to her sister.

"I'll see you before I go," Zeyde said before she pulled her into her arms and gave her a tight hug.

"Promise me you'll leave the moment he raises his hand to you. Promise me, Violet," Zeyde whispered so only she would hear.

Violet sniffled, then nodded. Her sister was so sure that the men of the village were as wicked as the Mahehkan men from their days of captivity, but she was wrong. Not all Mahehkan men were wicked. Some had fought for them. James and his men had freed many of the women over the years. They were good. A lot of them had died for their efforts, but still, those remaining had kept fighting. The fact that they were too few and up against almost insurmountable odds hadn't stopped them.

Joss was a good man, too. She couldn't say for sure about the other Komoro men, but Delana seemed madly in love with Khet. And none of the women she'd seen tonight had sported any bruises or injuries.

For now, that was enough for her.

Zeyde gave her one last hug before making her way through the crowd and out the door.

A huge lump clogged Violet's throat, and a small sob slipped past her lips as the door closed behind her sister.

"You okay?" Joss asked.

She turned and sniffled again, blinking her eyes fast. In an instant, Joss's arms opened and she didn't hesitate, stepping into them and resting her head on his chest. His arms came around her as the tears began to flow. This was supposed to be a celebration—a party—yet she'd done more crying since entering the pack house then she had in the past year.

"Shh." He stroked up and down her spine with his strong hands, holding her as gently as a newborn babe. "She'll come around. You'll see."

She was about to tell him that she wasn't so sure when the energy in the room shifted. Joss loosened his hold but didn't let her go, and she turned enough to see their Alpha make his way to the front of the room.

"Can I have your attention, please?" Argram said once he got there, and the crowd hushed immediately. "On behalf of myself and all members of the pack, we'd like to welcome all of our new pack mates to the Komoro village. My beautiful mate, Miga, and her numerous helpers have prepared this feast and celebration for us all. Enjoy."

Along the wall where the punch bowl and other drinks had been, a long table covered in plates and platters now stood. When had that happened? So engrossed in all the new people, and then her sister, she hadn't even noticed the undoubted activity it would have taken to set up such a thing, or even the luscious smells now filling the room.

As though her stomach had just caught on, it gave a hearty growl.

Joss looked down at her, then grinned. "Hungry?"

She thought about denying it, but he'd heard her, and she didn't want to start their relationship with untruths. "I am." If she were completely honest with herself, since she'd started eating regular meals— and snacks in between—she couldn't seem to get enough. She was always famished.

"Then let's get you some food." He led her to the end of the line forming at the banquet table, then handed her a plate when their turn came up. He stood behind her, taking what he wanted and pointing out his favorite dishes as he went, encouraging her to try whatever she wanted.

"There's no way I'm going to be able to eat all that," she exclaimed before she got anywhere near the end of the table. There was still so much food she wanted to try, and her plate was overflowing.

"I bet if we ask Miga, she'll let us take something home at the end of the night," Joss said with a smile. He'd obviously asked before and gotten rewarded for his efforts.

Each table had room for eight, so when people settled, she wasn't surprised to find that she and Joss were no longer alone. Even though he'd introduced them, Violet couldn't, for the life of her, remember everyone's names, but it didn't matter. The easy banter between men and women alike had her breathing easy and even laughing on occasion. All the while, Joss remained attentive to her every need, refreshing her drink and making sure she was comfortable.

After dessert had been served and she couldn't possibly eat another bite, the crowd thinned. Many remained seated, but others got up to clear the food and help clean up. A few made their way outside, but she suspected it was more to breathe in the fresh evening air than to leave.

Once the area was spotless again, the lights dimmed, and the music resumed a little louder than it had been. A soft ballad came on and Violet smiled. She didn't recognize the song, but it was pretty. It didn't take long before a couple made their way to the center of the room. Before she knew it, several other couples danced without a care in the world.

The song ended, and another began.

"Do you like to dance?" Joss asked her.

It had been so long since she'd done any dancing, but she used to love it. "I do. You?"

He gave her a pained look, then smiled again. "I do, but I'm not any good. In fact, Delana would say I've got two left feet. She tried showing me how years ago, but I'm not coordinated enough to make it happen."

"You can't possibly be that bad."

Joss's eyebrows rose. "You don't think so? I may have broken one of her toes once."

"Really?" She couldn't fathom Joss not being good at something.

He threw his head back and laughed. "No, I didn't do that, but I'm no good at it, that much is true."

Joss captured her hand and brought her fingers to his lips. "If you're brave enough to risk your toes, I'd love to dance with you."

Her heart skipped a beat. The music faded with the end of the song and then started up again with a new one. "I'd like that."

He stood, still holding her hand, then helped her to her feet. When they got to the makeshift dancefloor, he wrapped his arms around her and held her gaze. "If this gets to be too much for you, you'll let me know?" he asked.

"I will," she whispered, and he pulled her closer. Her breasts pressed lightly against his hard chest, and her rounded belly snugged against his flat one. She might have felt self-conscious except for the contented sigh he let out as he held her.

"This is nice," he told her as he began moving.

More than nice. It was right. Violet rested her head against his shoulder and let the music flow through her. Sure enough, they'd only taken a dozen steps before Joss's foot nudged up against her toes. He didn't step on them, but his foot was nowhere near where it should have been.

Violet tried hard. She did, but she couldn't help the little giggle that broke free.

They managed to make it about halfway through the song when Khet came waltzing by with Delana in his arms. Delana gave her a solemn look, mouthing "watch your toes" as she spun past.

That was it. The little giggle from before came back, quickly turning into a full-fledged laugh. Joss looked at her, a quizzical expression on his face, which only made her laugh harder. Then, in one ill-timed spin, his foot came down on top of hers. It was only a moment, and he had barely put any weight on it, but the look of sheer terror on his face had her howling.

"I'm so sorry. I told you I couldn't dance. Are you all right?"

The more he apologized, the harder she laughed. People were staring, but she couldn't help it. By the time she got herself under control, her cheeks hurt, and others around them were grinning.

Joss, on the other hand, stood there, looking at her. He wasn't smiling, but he wasn't frowning, either. Had she offended him? She nibbled on her bottom lip, trying to figure out what to say while keeping her giggles at bay.

He took the step needed to close the distance between them again and wrapped his arms loosely around her shoulders, maintaining eye contact. "Are you okay?" he asked. His chest rose and fell faster than it had before, and the warmth in his eyes grew hotter. His gaze flicked to her lips, and for an instant, she thought he might lean in and kiss her.

Her heart pounded. If there was any doubt left in her mind about her mate, his reaction to stepping so lightly on her toes sent those flying out the window. He wouldn't hurt her.

She took a steadying breath. "I'm fine," she whispered, then stepped on her tiptoes and pressed her lips to his.

# « CHAPTER 11 »

Heat infused Joss's entire body. Seeing Violet smiling had been like a balm to his soul all evening long, but hearing her laughter, seeing her happy...that had done something more. It had roused the wolf. It had wanted to get closer, to join in her fun. The fact that her laughter had risen from his literal misstep was of no consequence. He hadn't stomped down hard, but being that she was so delicate, he could have hurt her, and that was the last thing he ever wanted to do.

At some point, while she was laughing, the wolf's joy and playfulness had shifted. It had done well, keeping its distance as Violet healed, but she was everything that both he and the wolf wanted. She was theirs, and it wanted her now. It didn't care that they were in a public place, or that she wasn't ready for that kind of physical contact. The primal need to touch and taste rushed to the surface. With her in his arms, fighting the beast had been tough.

That was until she looked at him with those gorgeous brown eyes of hers, then lifted her lips to his. For a half second, he was too shocked to move, but when she leaned closer, pressing her sweet body against his, he'd lost the battle.

With a moan, he pulled her flush against him, returning her gentle kiss. He wanted to devour her, but the sane part in his mind held him back. Hard as it was, he'd let her call the shots.

After a moment, she surrendered a moan of her own, then probed at his lips with her tongue. He opened up for her, desperate for whatever she was offering. She deepened their kiss, her hands tightening around his waist.

He had no way of knowing how long they stood there, lost in each other. It could have been minutes—or maybe hours. He had no idea. All he knew was that his mate had given a part of herself to him, and he wanted to claim her.

When she finally pulled away, reality seeped back in. The music was still playing and people still danced. Although a few glanced in their direction with grins on their faces, no one commented or brought unnecessary attention to them, for which he was grateful. He doubted that Violet would have appreciated it.

Unwilling to let her go yet, he gave her a quick kiss on the tip of her nose. "If you're willing to give it another go, I think I can manage not to injure you if we keep dancing." The song playing wasn't the same one as before, but it was another slow one, so he'd get to hold on to her for a while longer. Just as well, if he had to step away, not only would Violet see it, but his erection would be on display for everyone present.

"I think it's safe enough," she said, smiling up at him.

Taking more care with his steps, he held her through that song and the next before bringing her back to the table, toes intact.

She sat and took a sip of her drink. "I know it's still early, but do you think we could go home soon? I'm getting a little tired," she said, not quite meeting his gaze.

*Crap.* Joss should have anticipated how much this would take out of her. Violet was still recuperating. He should have taken her home after the meal. Selfish as it was, he was glad he hadn't. Holding her like he had—kissing her—had been more than amazing. Her taste lingered on his tongue, and his body still hummed from the feel of her body against his.

"Yes, of course. I shouldn't have kept you out this long."

He helped her stand, and she wrapped her fingers around his. Not in the vise she'd held onto him with when they'd come in, but in the way a woman held her lover's hand.

He'd normally have gone out to find Miga and the others to thank them for all their hard work, but not tonight. He'd be sure to do that in the days to come, but right then, he had to take care of his mate. That meant getting her home so she could rest.

She stopped him with a small sigh as they walked past the new house on their way home.

"Do you think it will be ready before the baby comes?" she asked almost timidly.

"I think so. The outside is all but done now, and they're working on the rooms on the inside. I imagine we'll be able to move in a few weeks."

"Wow, they work fast."

He grinned at her and then glanced at her belly. "They know there's a deadline coming. They want to see us settled before the baby makes an appearance."

She nodded and stroked her hand over her stomach.

"I'd take you inside, but it's not safe in the dark. Heaven only knows what you'd step on."

Violet took a quick breath then looked away from him again, but not before he noticed the rosy hue on her cheeks. "That's okay."

"Is everything all right?" he asked. He sure as hell hoped she wasn't regretting their kiss.

"Yes, fine," she said breathlessly.

She wasn't panicking or pulling away from him, but something was off.

"Ready to go home?" she asked.

Home. In the past two days, he'd seen her come farther and farther out of her shell. She'd prepared food without being prompted and explored the house more, but nothing too extensive. Joy flooded his entire being at hearing her refer to it as their home. "Yes, let's go."

He flicked on the living room light as they walked in, expecting her to release his hand and go to the bedroom, but she didn't. She stayed with him as he went into the kitchen and poured them both a tall glass of juice. If she wanted to hold his hand, he sure as hell wasn't going to deny her. He loved the feel of her skin against his, even if it was just her palm and fingers.

Normally, he would have carried both glasses, but she still held his hand, so he handed one to her and took the other. "Want to sit on the couch for a while?" he asked.

"That would be nice."

He crossed an ankle over his opposing knee once they settled on the couch, then rested their joined hands on top. "What a night."

Violet took a deep breath and smiled. "It was something. That's for sure."

"I wish I had known your sister was in the village. I would have brought her to you much sooner."

Violet's eyes clouded for a moment but then cleared. "Let's not discuss that right now. I'm still digesting it myself."

The smile was still on her face, but the tension around her lips had him backtracking. He didn't want her worried or stressed out. "Okay. What would you like to talk about?"

Her gaze flicked to the floor, then quickly up again. "Us."

He waited for her to continue. After their kiss on the dance floor, this conversation could go either way. He hoped it would be in his favor.

"I know we've just met. And it seems like it's too fast, but I want us to get to know one another better," Violet said in a rush.

Her fingers tightened around his and he brought them up to his lips. "I'm all for that," he told her, then took a drink of his juice, becoming quiet again so she would continue.

"I think we should start sharing the bedroom."

The juice he'd swallowed nearly came rushing back out with his cough. Of all the things Violet could have said, that he hadn't expected.

Her eyes widened and she drew in a sharp breath. "Of course, if you don't want to—"

"I want to. Believe me, I do, Violet. But do you think you're ready for that? I don't mind sleeping on the couch." The idea of them sharing a bed had his blood rushing to his groin.

"I think it's important. I want to, and I'm ready for it," Violet insisted.

"I don't know, Violet. Being near you is like heaven for me. Sleeping in the same bed," he hesitated, "I just don't know if—"

"I know what you're getting at, and I've thought about it. I know you might react to me in a physical way, and it doesn't frighten me." The redness of her cheeks deepened, but she didn't look away.

Determination shone in her eyes. She had her head tilted up in that stubborn way he was already learning to love. If this is what she wanted, then so be it. "Okay."

# « CHAPTER 12 »

Breathing had never been this difficult. For a second, she thought Joss was going to deny her, and she hadn't been prepared for that rejection—not in the least. One of the things she thought she knew about men was that they usually let their libidos make decisions for them. She'd all but offered her body up to him on a platter, and he'd hesitated.

Another woman might have been hurt by it, or even afraid that he was refusing her because of her pregnant state, but this was Joss. He'd never given her any indication that he was anything but considerate and kind. She would chalk this up to more of his thoughtfulness. Besides, she wasn't an idiot. His cock hadn't lied as they'd kissed or when they'd danced. It had been hard, willing, and ready. Now she had to convince her mate to use it.

For the first time since they'd left the pack house, she disentangled her fingers from his and stood.

There was no point in pretending. She wanted him. "I'm going to get ready for bed. Will you join me?" she asked, her heart hammering away as she waited for his answer.

For a second, it looked like he might protest again, but then she lifted her hand, silencing him.

"Please, don't deny me. Unless you don't want me." She looked down at his crotch, and sure enough, it was pressing against his zipper "Don't push me away. I know what I want. I know what I'm capable of handling. Let me make that decision for myself."

***

Joss could barely hear Violet's words over the pounding of his heart. She wasn't only offering to share the bed. She wanted to share her body. And even though it was something he desperately wanted, he couldn't help the anxiety from surging forward. It was too soon. Their fragile bond could so easily be damaged or even severed. All it would take would be one mistake on his part, and they'd be at the starting line again.

But what choice did he have? Lie to her? That wasn't going to happen. He couldn't look into her eyes and tell her he didn't want her.

"I'll be in there shortly," he found himself saying. Then with a little smile, Violet turned and headed to the back of the house, her cute little pink dress flowing around her legs with each sway of her hips. Yeah, he was a goner.

He listened from his spot on the couch as she got ready for bed, then made her way to the bedroom, expecting to hear the door click shut behind her, but she left it open. He gave her a couple of minutes to get settled before following.

When he entered the room, Violet sat on her knees in the center of the bed with one of his T-shirts covering her body from his sight, bathed in the light of the lamp she'd left lit behind her. He'd bet that if she stood, the hem would go halfway down her thighs. With her hands by her side, she looked the perfect image of innocence and vixen. Her long hair fell around her shoulders, and with the light shining at her back, she looked like she had a halo. His very own angel. Her breasts jutted out before her, and her nipples poked at the soft white fabric keeping them from his sight. He came closer, watching her every step of the way. If she so much as flinched, he swore he'd stop and head back to the couch. Too much was riding on this.

He grabbed the back of his shirt in his fist and pulled it over his head. Her eyes widened, but she didn't look away. Her soft lips parted, and she looked down his chest to his waistband, then up again, swallowing when she reached his face again.

Damn. It was hard enough to be in there with Violet, but to have her looking at him as though she wanted to devour him strained his tenuous control.

When he reached for the snap of his jeans, her gaze followed his hands, and she wet her lips. Try as he might, he couldn't hold back the moan. She was sexy as hell, and she wasn't even trying. Maybe that was part of what made it so arousing. She didn't even know how much of a temptation she was sitting there all covered up, yet so exposed.

"Don't stop," she whispered.

Had he? Bracing himself—for what, he wasn't sure— he popped the snap, then lowered the zipper. There was no way he could hide his cock. It was so full and hard that it ached. It didn't matter that he had underwear on, there was no disguising his erection.

Her gaze stayed glued to him as he stepped out of his jeans and tossed them to the chair in the opposite corner.

"Are you sure about this?" he asked as he stepped to the edge of the bed. Leaving would be hell, but he'd rather do that than hurt her in any way.

She nodded quickly. "I'm sure."

Those two little, breathy words went straight to his groin.

When she scrambled back toward the headboard, he thought she'd had a change of heart or the panic had returned. He braced himself for the hurt and mistrust he was sure would be shining in her eyes, but when she looked at him again, her eyes shone, not with recrimination, but with passion. Violet pulled the sheets down, waiting for him to join her. "I don't know which side of the bed you prefer," she finally said.

Which side of the bed? That was her biggest concern? Joss sat on the edge, facing her. "I'll be happy on either side as long as you're comfortable," he assured her.

Her smile grew and she scooted farther back, leaving him the side closest to the door. It made sense. With him lying between her and the door, it was the safest place, instantly making it his preferred spot, as well.

## « CHAPTER 13 »

If Joss didn't get a move on, Violet thought she might scream. The fact that he was so concerned about her reaction to having sex with him made her all the surer that it was what she wanted. She hadn't been a virgin when Karak had taken her. She'd known pleasure with a man before. The fact that she hadn't known it while in captivity didn't negate that. And it didn't mean she equated sex to the horrors forced on her by her captors.

Joss sighed then took a deep breath. He was going to try to talk her out of it. The worry in his eyes didn't lie.

Before he could say a word, she reached for the hem of the T-shirt she wore, hesitating for a moment at the idea of showing her mate her swollen belly. Joss's chest rose and fell with his quick breaths as he let his gaze rove over her. The small appreciative noise coming from his throat gave her the courage she needed to bring the shirt the rest of the way up, then off.

Her heart leaped as he devoured her with his gaze. Her nipples tightened, and a sweet throb pulsed between her legs.

"Jesus, Violet," he all but growled. "You're so fucking gorgeous I can barely keep my wolf contained."

The thought of him losing control should have scared the crap out of her, but all it did was make the throb beat faster in her clit. If he didn't do something soon, maybe she'd have to tackle him instead.

Joss shifted to his hands and knees and crawled across the expanse of the bed between them, looking his fill the entire time. "I want to touch you, Violet. Will you let me do that?" he asked.

*Yes. Hell yes.* Violet wanted to scream the words, but only managed a nod.

He adjusted the pillow, positioning it under her head better from where it had gone askew when she'd scrambled to the top to pull the blankets down. Bringing his hand up, he stroked a finger gently along her jaw, then lowered his head and pressed a soft kiss to the corner of her mouth.

Cupping her cheek, he turned her face, claiming her mouth, moaning when she opened up to him. *Yes, that. More*, her she-wolf whispered.

Violet's heart pounded. The beast inside her rarely communicated anymore. Some days, she'd swear it wasn't there at all, but heat seeped from her core, filling every inch of her. More than ever, she wanted to rub herself all over Joss, and she didn't have to guess what was happening. The wolf wanted her mate, and Violet was more than happy to comply. When Joss would have pulled back, she gave a little growl.

His lips against her tightened in a grin. He sucked her bottom lip between his and gave it a little tug between his teeth.

"May I?" he asked again as his hand stroked a path from her shoulder to the top of her left breast.

"Please," was all she could manage.

When his hand curved around her and his palm grazed her sensitive nipple, she arched into the touch.

"More," she begged.

Joss stiffened. "I don't want to go too fast. I don't want to scare you."

He still wasn't sure, but she was, and she had a feeling that showing him she wasn't afraid would go a lot further than telling him. So Violet reached for his other hand and brought it to her other breast. "That feels amazing, Joss. I can't wait for you to kiss them. I need you to—so bad," she said as she thrust deeper into the touch.

He groaned and squeezed both breasts, kneading her flesh. Each time he did, her nipple scraped his palm, driving her to the point of madness, but he didn't rush. When she thought she'd have to push him again, he changed the way he held her and rolled her nipples between his thumbs and fingers. He closed his eyes and moaned at the same time she did.

"Yes. Please, Joss" The pulse in her clit throbbed hard, and all he'd done was play with her breasts and nipples.

Without saying a word, he opened his eyes and looked straight into hers, raising an eyebrow in silent question. Violet nodded quickly. He licked his lips, and when she whimpered and arched her back, thrusting her chest higher, he finally lowered his mouth to her nipple.

Her moan started off soft but grew louder as he increased the suction on her breast. It had been so long since she'd had an orgasm, she might go off with nothing more than he was doing. It felt that good.

She hadn't realized she'd moved at all until she felt the soft strands of his hair between her fingers. She was holding him to her breast. He flicked his tongue over the glistening peak, then sucked it between his lips again.

She inadvertently gave a tug as the pleasure rushed through her, zinging from her nipple to her clit and back again. Joss's lips curved into a smile, but he didn't let go. Looking down at her mate, his mouth on her body, the pleasure he was bringing her was almost more than she could take.

"I need more, Joss, please," she panted. The ache between her legs grew. She squirmed on the bed, trying to squeeze her legs together, desperate for relief, but it wasn't enough.

He released her and grazed his teeth first along the swell of her breast, then around her already aching nipple. "Tell me what you want, Violet."

Heat rushed to her cheeks, but she was beyond caring. She needed relief, and Joss could help her. "My clit. I need some pressure down there, please."

"You want my hand or my mouth?" he asked, his voice deeper, raspier than she'd ever heard it.

"Your hand—your fingers—please." She didn't wait for him to ask, spreading her legs apart enough that he could not only see every bit of her, but he could easily reach. Violet held her breath as he stroked his hand down her belly, cupping the hardness in his hand for a moment with a smile playing on his lips, then moved lower. The heat of his palm reached her first, and she moaned before he touched her. She wouldn't last long. She'd have to make it up to him afterward, because right then, nothing could stop her from reaching for the pleasure he promised.

He slid one finger down her slit, then up again, circling her swollen clit before trailing down again. Violet couldn't contain her moan. She lifted her hips off the bed, helplessly demanding more, but he kept the strokes light.

"Do you want me to suck on your nipples again, Violet?" he asked with a growl.

"God yes, please," she begged. She hadn't been aware that she still held his hair in her fist until he lowered his mouth to her again and her hand followed.

The moment he had her nipple between his lips, he sucked—hard. At the same instant, he flicked his finger over her clit, then back again. Her scream came from deep within as pleasure coursed through her.

She was so close. Her hips bucked against his hand as Joss continued his onslaught. He pulled away only long enough to capture the other nipple and give her another few swipes, bringing her all the way to the edge of her climax without toppling her over.

Her lungs burned as her ragged breaths couldn't keep up with her body's demands. Her legs shook, and the pulse in her clit throbbed in a heavy beat, each one making her blood pump faster and faster in her veins.

Joss pulled away and nipped at the tender flesh of her breast, making her jump, then moan as the sting morphed into pleasure. He slowed his fingers, teasing her entrance before sliding up again. When he came back to her, he circled, then paused, his finger poised for entry. She closed her eyes and tried to thrust her hips up to meet him, but he wouldn't let her.

"Tell me you want me inside you, Violet. That you want my fingers," he said, his voice rough—barely human.

"God yes, please, please, please," she chanted as he bit the skin just below her nipple, making her whimper and her pussy tighten around emptiness.

He captured the taut peak again, and then slid his finger all the way in.

Violet gasped at the sweet intrusion, then moaned. The walls of her pussy clenched his digit as he retreated then slid it home again. "More," she whispered, hardly able to voice the word.

When he pulled out again, he came back in with a second finger, and her breath caught in her throat.

"Yes, yes, yes," she said, each word coming out louder than the last. Deep in her psyche, a small voice told her to be quiet. That noise was not tolerated, but she shoved it aside. It was too good. She couldn't stop.

When he curled his fingers and stroked deep inside her, she had no hope of avoiding it. Her orgasm crashed over her as pleasure overtook. Her heart pounded, and her pussy gripped his fingers in a stranglehold as he continued driving them into her. He slowed his movements as she came back into her body, finally pulling them out when she was limp on the mattress in front of him.

Joss lay next to her and pulled her close. She would have to move—do something—very soon, but her body wasn't quite ready. All the strength in her muscles had melted into a puddle of sexual bliss. Once she found the strength again, she'd take care of him. Violet lay her head on Joss's shoulder and closed her eyes. She'd rest for a minute, and then she'd see to his pleasure.

## « CHAPTER 14 »

Joss lay there for a while, listening to Violet breathe. He'd known the instant she'd fallen asleep. Her breaths had lengthened, and her body had all but melted into him. He couldn't stop smiling. Giving Violet pleasure had driven his wolf wild with want, but also satisfied him in a way nothing else could.

The fact that the wolf had been so close to the surface had worried him, though he'd tried not to show it. Had she put those delicate little hands of hers—or heaven forbid, those sensuous lips—on his body, he would have been a goner. It was bad enough that he'd almost given her a claiming bite when he'd bitten her breast, but the way he'd been feeling, he wouldn't have been able to be gentle in taking her. So when she'd fallen asleep with her head on his shoulder, it had been a relief.

With a contented sigh, he tightened his arm around her and finally closed his eyes. They'd figure out their dynamics in due time. For now, he was happy that she trusted him—if not with her heart yet, at least with her body—and that he got to sleep with her snuggled at his side.

A deep moan filtered through Joss's sleep-fogged mind. He'd never had a more vivid dream. Violet's tongue flicked over the tip of his cock, tasting the wetness pearling at the tip. He thrust his hips involuntarily toward her lips. He moaned again, bringing him closer to wakefulness. If he wasn't dreaming, then Violet was doing a lot more than sleeping. His body stiffened as he opened his eyes. With the pale morning light streaming through the bedroom window, she looked like an angel.

She had her lips poised above the head of his cock and was looking up at him with passion shining in her eyes. "Good morning," she whispered before she took the head into her mouth.

Joss grasped the sheet on either side of his body and moaned. Pleasure pounded through him, pooling in his balls, making them ache with the need to release. "Violet, what are you doing?" he asked, his voice raspier than he would have liked.

She pulled off him with a pop, then gave him another lick before meeting his gaze. "I'm taking what's mine," she said. She looked at him, her eyes determined, almost daring him to deny her.

He was no fucking idiot. He was hers. Just as Violet was his. And if she wanted his cock in her mouth first thing in the morning, who was he to deny her?

"Fuck, that feels good," he encouraged as he rested his head against his pillow again.

She didn't hesitate, bringing that warm, wet tongue of hers back to his shaft, licking all the way down to his balls and up again. By the time she made it back to the crown, he was gripping the sheet so tightly that he heard a soft rip, but he didn't care.

She took her time, driving him crazy with each swipe of her tongue, each lick, and every gentle nibble she placed upon his flesh.

Not wanting to come too fast, he'd stopped watching her exploration shortly after she'd started, but when the mattress shifted and her heated mouth left his body, his eyes sprang open. She looked all the way up, a small, uncertain smile upon her lips, as she draped a leg over his thighs, bringing her pussy within inches of his raging hard cock.

"Is this okay?" she asked, her voice less confident than it had been before.

He grunted, barely comprehending that she'd felt the need to ask. "Fuck, yes," he said a little too emphatically.

Her smile broadened, and she brought herself up so that she was poised above him. She tried to reach him, to hold him steady for her to take him, but her belly got in the way. She gave a frustrated huff.

"I've got it," he told her as he reached down and held his cock. The pulsing beat in his shaft mirrored the one in his balls. He couldn't wait to feel her flesh surrounding him.

Violet adjusted her hips and lowered herself over him one inch at a time until he was fully sheathed. Her heat and tightness all but strangled his cock.

Joss groaned as the pleasure spiked through him. After having her glorious lips on his cock for so long, there was no way he was going to last. Rather than pull his hand away once she was in place, he brought it down between them. When she lifted herself over him and then came back down, he stroked her clit, making her gasp.

Her heavy breasts swayed with her slow movement at first, bouncing faster as she picked up the pace. All the while, he stroked her clit, moaning each time he did when her pussy tightened its grip on his cock.

His balls drew up tight, and the pulse pounded through his shaft. He flicked her clit faster— harder—as Violet rode him. She threw her head back and lifted her hands to her breasts, tweaking her nipples as her moans grew longer and louder. He'd never seen anyone sexier in all his life. Her breasts, round and heavy in her hands, made him want to have another taste. Rather than detract from her beauty, her belly made her look more feminine. Add to that being able to watch his cock disappear into the heaven of her body, and he couldn't hold back.

He grabbed hold of her hips, and when she came down over him again, he speared into her. Her scream filled the room as her pussy clenched around him. With a final thrust, he drove himself home, filling her with everything he had as she milked him with her climax.

His cock was still jerking inside her when she came forward. Her weight pressed against his chest for nothing more than a moment before she pushed herself up a couple of inches. She looked into his eyes. "You're mine," she declared, before leaning down again and biting his chest.

Fiery pleasure lashed through him again, making him cry out as the mating claim took hold. The wolf part of his soul howled its pleasure as the human part basked in the sensations rushing through him. He tightened his arms around her as his need to return her bite flooded him.

She stiffened in his arms but didn't lift her head from where she'd rested against his chest, right above his heart where his wound was already healing. "Not yet, I'm not ready," she whispered. A small patch of dampness pooled on his skin beneath her cheek.

"Hey, it's okay," he whispered, but he heard the muffled sob she tried to hide. After everything she'd been through, it was amazing that she'd allowed him near her at all. That she'd extended her trust to him at all was a miracle. So he'd have to wait a while before he could claim her. So what? She needed the time, and he sure as hell would give it to her.

She sniffled and shook her head. "I'm sorry."

He tightened his arms around her and held her close. "I'm not. Not even a little. It'll happen, but not until the time is right."

She lifted her head and gave him a wobbly smile. "You're not mad?"

He brushed the hair out of her face and gave her his most reassuring smile. "Not in the least. You've honored me with your trust. You've given me the pleasure of your body. You've even staked your claim on me, binding me to you forever. So I haven't bitten you yet. That's okay. We'll do things our way. In our own time. No one said the mating bites had to be exchanged together. And it doesn't make it any less wonderful because they aren't."

Violet wiped her cheeks. "You're sure?"

"Positive," he told her and leaned up to kiss her nose. "Now, let's get a bit more rest. The sun has barely risen, and I'm not ready to get out of bed yet." He didn't tell her that with her body still surrounding him, he may never want to get out of bed again.

She smiled at him. "Me neither," she admitted as she snuggled closer.

Reaching over, he pulled the blankets to cover them both. The last thing he wanted was for Violet to get off him, so when she stayed right where she was, he wrapped his arms around her and closed his eyes.

## « CHAPTER 15 »

As much as he hated to do it, Joss forced himself out of bed a few hours later. He'd promised the crew at the house that he'd be by to lend a hand today, and he was already late. It was bad enough that he'd left them to do the bulk of the work while he stayed home and tended to Violet's needs. Of course, they all understood and encouraged him to do so, but he wanted to have a hand in building their home. Put his stamp on it, so to speak.

So after a quick shower and a few not-so-quick kisses, he'd packed a sandwich and left Violet at home. If he were visiting the site, he'd have taken her with him, but he'd be there for a while, and she'd get bored, not to mention uncomfortable. No, it was best for her not to come. Besides, she'd mentioned going for a short walk to take in some of the autumn colors before the snow began to fall. It would do her good to regain some of her independence.

He hadn't mentioned that one or two of the men would be following close by if she wandered outside of the village. She wouldn't see or even hear them unless they purposely made their presence known. It wasn't a rule, but with the Mahehkan wolves hanging around the Komoro territory, it didn't hurt to be a little extra cautious.

Joss was busy hammering away inside the house when Argram showed up, his scowl deeper than usual. "What's up?" he asked the Alpha, not bothering with pleasantries.

"We've been approached by the Mahehkans. Their leader wants to meet with me." Argram snarled through clenched teeth.

"So, let them come. The bastard won't stand a chance in a challenge against you."

Argram growled. "It's not me he's coming for."

Joss's hammer stopped mid-swing. He didn't have to ask who *he* was. "What do you mean?" Fury filled his entire being. That bastard had better not be coming for Violet.

Argram gritted his teeth so hard he had to have chipped a tooth. "The one they name Karak says his mate is held here against her will."

"No," Joss yelled the word. "Like fuck he's going to get his hands on her ever again. I will kill him first."

Argram grunted his agreement. The other men had stopped their work and now surrounded them. "Let him come," one of them said as he gave Joss a brotherly pat on the back. "He's on borrowed time anyway."

"I don't have to allow him passage into the village," Argram stated.

"It's time to end this. Let Karak in."

\*\*\*

Violet took a deep breath and wrapped the sweater she'd brought with her tighter around her body. The days were getting cooler, and there was a definite crispness to the air that meant only one thing. Snow soon. The leaves had mostly fallen, but the scent of the season still lingered in the air. She couldn't remember the last time she'd been free to go for a walk for no other reason than to enjoy the forest around her.

She'd gone a mile, two at most, when she heard a twig snap to her left. She whipped her gaze in that direction and just about screamed when she found Zeyde standing only a few feet away from her. Lost in her thoughts, she hadn't even heard her sister's approach.

"Zeyde, you scared the crap out of me."

Her sister shrugged, but the small quirk of her lips told her that she wasn't serious. "Why are you out walking alone?"

Violet looked around but didn't see anyone else. "Because I can?"

Zeyde shook her head and smiled for real this time. "It's not safe."

Violet grinned. "Sure it is. I have an escort."

Zeyde's eyebrows rose. "You noticed?"

It was her turn to smile. "Of course, I noticed. I might have been daydreaming when you showed up, but I wasn't when I left the village. I will admit, they're pretty good at hiding, though."

Zeyde looked at her booted feet. "So, are you going to leave with me?"

She shook her head. "No. I'm not. My home is with the Komoro pack now."

Her sister gave her head a shake. "Do you think he's going to want to keep you around after the baby?

That he's going to want to raise another wolf's child? Think about this, Violet. What man would do that?"

A small sliver of doubt sliced through her, but she squashed it. "Joss would. He's a good man, Zeyde. You may not be able to look past what those assholes did to us, but I can. I refuse to live in fear or deny myself happiness because of them. I won't let them win, and you shouldn't, either."

Violet spun on her heels, intent on walking back to the village—back to Joss—when a flash of brown and gray fur sprang from the brush straight toward them.

"Run, Violet," Zeyde screamed at her as the wolf leaped. In an instant, her sister shifted, shoving her aside as she jumped to intercept. Cold dread filled her. She'd never forget that gray and brown coat or the nasty scent of the bastard who had fathered her child. Karak had come for her. Zeyde circled him, snarling long and loud. What was she doing? She was no match for Karak. She'd get herself killed.

"Zeyde, no," Violet screamed, but her sister ignored her.

Karak lunged, and Zeyde met him halfway, teeth gnashing and claws slicing through flesh. Droplets of blood splattered around. Fear freezing her in place, Violet could only watch as the monster who'd held her captive knocked her sister to the ground. Growls erupted around her, and a moment later, a much larger wolf had Karak pinned with its massive jaw around his neck. Another wolf, equally large, paced between her and Zeyde, keeping both women in its sights as it looked for more threats.

Only when it seemed satisfied there were none did he come to her. He whined and gently nudged her with his nose, urging her to get moving. Violet tried to take a step, but her knees shook so hard she thought she might fall flat on her face. Karak was there. He had found her. Had it not been for the Komoro men, Zeyde would be dead, and Karak would have taken her.

Try as she might, Violet couldn't take her eyes off Karak. He lay there, docile as could be, but she knew there was nothing submissive about him. She almost wished he'd put up a fight and give the other male a reason to end his life, but he was too smart for that. No, he'd bide his time, and when he thought he could win, he'd come back. He wouldn't stop.

The wolf nudged her again, and this time, with Zeyde's plaintive whine, she was able to move. She rushed over to her sister and ran her fingers through her soft brown fur. "Are you okay?" she asked, her voice shaky. There were no bones poking out anywhere, but when Violet lifted her hands, blood covered them.

"Come on, we have to get you back to the village," Violet told her, but Zeyde lay there, panting. The fur on her head was damp with perspiration. "Shit."

What the hell was she supposed to do? She couldn't carry her sister all the way back. Maybe, had she not been so far along, but at more than seven months, they'd never make it. Her heart pounded, but she had no choice. She faced the huge silver grey wolf still standing guard. "You have to carry her," she told him. Then, realizing the demand she'd made, she tried again. "Please, can you help us?"

It spared her a glance then his gaze snapped back to Zeyde. His growl came fast and sharp, making Violet stumble back. What the hell had she done? "Please, no, don't hurt her," she begged.

The wolf's body shook, then he threw his head back and howled—or rather roared—long and loud. She'd never heard a wolf howl like that. Violet took a tentative step toward her sister, giving him a wide berth. She had to get Zeyde away from him.

Another thundering roar came at her from the direction of the village, then another from somewhere behind them. That one was close—too close. Her heart hammered against her ribs, and her lungs burned for air. They were Komoro men, but she didn't even know who was hiding beneath all that fur. For all she knew, they weren't any nicer than Karak. No, that was crazy. The wolf had been protective of her until it had scented Zeyde. It didn't make sense.

"It's okay. I'm just going to take my sister and go," she whispered so softly she couldn't be sure he'd heard. She took another step toward her, and the wolf's lips pulled back in a silent snarl. Okay, so that wasn't going to happen.

Violet stood with her feet rooted to the ground. She didn't let her gaze stray from the beast, but she didn't make eye contact, either. She couldn't see how any wolf that size would see her as a threat, but she wasn't taking any chances.

Relief poured into her as the sounds of men shouting and wolves pounding the forest floor reached her ears. They'd be able to help. They'd know how to deal with this. The wolf had been protective of her until it had sniffed out her sister.

A familiar scent filtered to her on the cool breeze. Joss. He was coming. Others were, too. Unable to hold herself up any longer, she sank to her knees as relief poured into her. Joss would know what to do. He'd keep her and Zeyde safe.

## « CHAPTER 16 »

Joss had already been following Violet's scent into the forest when he'd heard Rennan's roar up ahead. The call had been answered immediately by their pack mates, but Joss didn't bother responding. He'd only ever heard the summoning roar a couple of times, and each time, the threats to their people had been great. To hear it again sent a shiver racing down his spine and made him run harder than he'd ever run before. Violet's scent was strong. She was in danger, and he had to get to her. Had he not been so close, he would have shifted, but stopping to strip would have slowed him down. He had to get to her.

Joss crashed into the small clearing in time to see Violet stumbling to her knees a few feet away from Rennan. The wolf's body was taut, and his teeth bared. He was barely keeping from going into a rage from the looks of it.

He came closer, slowing his step. "It's okay, Violet. I'm here," he said loud enough for both her and Rennan to hear. Fury rushed to the surface as her small sob reached his ears. Was she hurt? The coppery scent of blood filled his nose, but it wasn't Violet's. It was close, but not the same. He looked past Rennan's massive body, spotting the small brown wolf lying on the ground. Zeyde. It had to be. The smell was too close to be anything but family. What the hell had happened?

Another growl from close to the treeline a dozen feet away drew his attention. Khet had a wolf pinned. Fucking Mahehkan. He suppressed his growl, needing to get to Violet. "Thank you for protecting my mate, Rennan. I can take over here," he said.

Rennan grunted in his native language, then paced closer to Zeyde. He watched, ready to defend Violet's sister if need be, but when Rennan whimpered and poked her gently with his nose, then licked at her muzzle, Joss knew he had nothing to worry about.

"Are you okay, love?" he asked Violet, crouching down in front of her.

Violet looked at him, then at her sister before shaking her head. Her bottom lip wobbled, and her eyes shone with moisture.

"Are you hurt?" He'd strip her down and examine her himself if need be, but he'd give her the chance to speak up first.

She shook her head again. "N-no. He's come for me," she said in a strangled whisper as though it made all the sense in the world.

The tension he'd released when he'd found her safe rushed back, making his muscles bunch and his skin burn with the effort to keep from shifting. "That's Karak?" he asked, his voice garbled.

She swallowed hard, then nodded. Joss made a move to stand, but she snaked her hand out, reaching for his arm. Her fingers trembled so hard he could feel it against his skin as she clutched onto him. "No, don't. Please." Only the panic in her eyes kept him where he was. If it weren't for her, he'd already be tearing into the bastard, ripping him to shreds.

The only thing that allowed him to turn his back on them was the knowledge that Khet would never let the enemy go. As much as he wanted to kill the bastard, that wasn't what Violet needed. And if he caught another glimpse of the male who'd abused his mate, he wouldn't be able to keep his wolf contained, no matter how much Violet pleaded.

He opened his arms wide, and she flung herself into them. She buried her face in his neck and hot, wet tears streamed from her cheeks onto his shoulder. "Zeyde is hurt, and that male won't let me near her," she finally managed to get out.

"It's okay. Rennan's got her. He won't let anything happen to her," he told her, his voice much calmer than he'd expected it would be. If his suspicion was right, the two were fated. Nothing else would have elicited that kind of response from the man.

Violet peeked over his shoulder to where Zeyde lay, and her body sagged against his a little. Whatever she'd seen, she wasn't quite as frightened.

A growl so deep and angry it could only come from Argram filled the clearing. He bounded to the center, assessing the situation with eyes that missed nothing. He went to Zeyde first, sniffing, then grunting something at Rennan, who stood there, unmoving.

The instant he went near, Khet placed a huge paw on the other wolf's chest and released his throat. He grunted and coughed, communicating with the Alpha in a way Joss couldn't begin to comprehend.

As soon as Khet had released Karak from his jaw, the bastard tried to get out from under his grip. One snarl from Argram stopped his movement cold. Argram responded to Khet, then paced back to where Rennan was. He didn't bother hiding from the women as he shifted, but it didn't matter. Zeyde's eyes were closed, and Violet had her face buried in Joss's neck.

"Delana is here. She'll examine Zeyde. You so much as snarl at her, and you'll lose more than a little fur," he threatened. The fact that Khet would be on him in an instant should have been threat enough, but to have the Alpha issue the order, there was no way the man would so much as look at Lanie funny.

"It's safe, you can come," Argram called over his shoulder.

A moment later, Delana came into the clearing. Her gaze sought out her mate first, then went straight to Zeyde. She knelt on the ground next to the she-wolf. "This is going to hurt a little," she warned the female. The hair on Rennan's scruff rose, but he didn't move. He didn't utter a sound.

She made quick work of examining Zeyde. "From the looks of it, she's lost a lot of blood. I'd guess a blood vessel was damaged, but her body is healing fast. She's not bleeding now, but I imagine she's weak. She'll be okay, Ren," she finally reassured him, and in the process, Violet, as well.

Argram grunted, and for the first time, Joss realized he hadn't come alone. At least a half dozen wolves littered the forest around them. "Take your mates home. Khet, you can bring our guest to the village. I'd like to speak with him when I return. He had better hope I don't find any more intruders on our land while I'm out. It would bode much better for him if I didn't," he snarled before he shifted again.

As much as he wanted to deal with Karak himself, Joss wouldn't. There was no way he was leaving Violet in the care of anyone else.

## « CHAPTER 17 »

Violet couldn't stop shaking. Karak was in the village—somewhere—probably sweet-talking someone into letting him go. But he wouldn't leave. Now that he was in the village, he'd find a way to get to her. To take her away. She'd seen him in action more than once. His charm had fooled many unsuspecting females, and it wasn't until it was too late that they discovered the monster he truly was— the one she knew him to be.

After Argram had given his orders, he'd gone into the forest with his men, and Joss had taken her home. She couldn't quite remember if she walked or if he carried her, but she was soaking in a tub full of hot water, yet shivering as though the coldest winter wind blew against her skin.

She nearly jumped out of the tub when a soft rap on the bathroom door came moments later.

"Can I come in?" Joss asked.

She had purposely left the door open a few inches so she could hear him and know he was close, so having him come in was more than fine. It meant he was even closer. "Yes."

He sat on the edge of the tub, looking her straight in the eye. "Listen, I know you won't want to hear this, but I have to say it. Argram will be back soon, and we'll both be needed at the village center to tell him what happened out there. I'd do it for you, but I wasn't there for most of it, so he'll want to hear it straight from you."

She'd known this would happen, but hearing it confirmed set her heart racing.

"I'll be right there with you."

She wished she could say no, but that wasn't an option. "Thank you."

Joss leaned in and gave her a soft kiss on the lips. "I'd do anything for you, love. This is a drop in the bucket."

She gave him what she hoped was a reassuring smile, but by the look he gave her, she didn't think she'd managed all that well. "I'll be out in a minute."

"Take your time. Argram will understand," he said as he stood and reached for the door.

When he stepped into the hallway, she pulled the plug. Waiting wouldn't make things any easier. As much as she wished it would all go away, it wouldn't. She needed to do this so she could move on with her life.

She dressed quickly, putting on the warmest sweater she could find, and pulled her hair into a ponytail. Karak had hated for her to have her hair tied back. He liked having something to hang on to. Something to use to pull and inflict pain. Not anymore.

Joss waited for her in the living room, his face somber. "Ready?"

"Not hardly, but I'll be okay."

As soon as they were on the sidewalk, he took her hand, entwining their fingers, and she was glad for that little bit of contact. She wasn't in the mood to talk, and he didn't press her for conversation. They were almost at the village center when the first snowflakes drifted down, melting on contact.

Had the situation been different, she would have marveled at it, but she barely noticed the cool spots on her skin.

Their pack mates, men and women alike, surrounded the area, providing an arena of sorts, and Violet's steps faltered. "They're expecting a challenge, aren't they?" she asked Joss, her heart racing.

"Yes."

She looked at him and drew to a stop, halting him along with her. She waited for him to look at her. "You're going to have to fight him?"

"Have to? No. Will I? Yes," he told her.

"No. You can't. Karak doesn't fight fair," Violet all but screamed. People all around them looked at her as though she'd grown a second head, but she didn't care. "You can't fight him. Please, say you won't."

"Violet," he said with a sigh. "I would do anything for you. Anything. But I will not decline his challenge when he throws it out there. And he will. He wants you. And there's no way in hell I'll ever let him get his hands on you again. Never."

"He'll kill you."

Joss shook his head. "He'll try."

"But—"

"I'm not afraid of the challenge, love. Be brave for me one more time, and when it's over, you'll be free of Karak once and for all."

He looked so certain of himself, so sure that he would be victorious, that she couldn't deny him. "Okay. Don't die."

He brought her hands to his lips and kissed her knuckles. "I won't," he assured her as he brought her through the crowd and into the clearing to join Argram and Wesken in the center.

Argram inclined his head toward him and Violet but remained silent. Moments later, the crowd parted, letting Khet and a struggling Karak, now in human form and ill-fitting clothes, into the ring.

Varying shades of red, blue, and dark purple colored his skin.

"What happened to his face?" the Alpha asked.

"He tried to run and smashed into a tree. With his face. Twice," Khet said, not bothering to hide his bleeding knuckles.

Argram's eyebrows rose.

"He may have run more than twice. I lost count," Khet continued.

The Alpha's face turned a deeper shade of pink, and his lips tightened as though he was suppressing laughter. "That's unfortunate," he finally said.

"Karak, of the Mahehkan pack, you've trespassed on my land and led seven others to do the same. You attacked my pack sister. What defense for your actions can you give me to spare your life for those infractions alone?" Argram said loud enough for all to hear.

Karak struggled against Khet's hold, glaring straight at Violet. "Tell this prick to let go of me. As Alpha of the Mahehkan pack, I deserve a measure of respect."

Argram's expression didn't change, but the energy in the air spiked higher. "Let him go. If he tries to run, find him another tree."

Karak blanched but settled when Khet released him.

"Alpha of the Mahehkan pack. Now that's interesting. The old Alpha—the one I killed, making me the rightful Alpha—wasn't a nice man. I wonder, are you any better? Do you deserve the title?" Argram stalked toward the man, and Karak took a step back.

"I will lead my pack to greatness, but I need the Mahehkans you stole from me to do it," he pressed.

"Each member of *my* pack is here of their free will. As for the men who had been trespassing along with you, they will be held until I deem them safe to set free."

Karak sneered and looked at her again. "It's my mate I want. You can kill the rest of them," he spat.

Violet knew it was coming, but hearing the words had her heart beating so fast she couldn't catch her breath. Joss gave her hand a reassuring squeeze.

"Your mate isn't in this village," the Alpha insisted.

Karak stupidly shot him a furious look. "She's. Right. Fucking. There."

Argram looked over at her and Joss and shook his head. "You're wrong. Violet is Joss's mate."

Karak gave her a wicked smile, showing his crooked teeth. "Who's bite do you bear, Violet?" he asked her with a sneer.

Joss's growl came out of nowhere. She'd thought he was as calm as the Alpha was, but with one look in his direction, she knew the truth. Lines of tension bracketed his mouth. The hand that wasn't holding hers was fisted tightly at his side.

"It's okay, *darling*, you don't have to say it. I'll say it for you. I know how you like to keep your fucking mouth shut," he threatened.

Joss released her hand and lunged at him. Had it not been for Khet pulling him back, he would have succeeded in reaching him.

"That's right, lover boy. You've been fucking my mate. And I'm taking her back. Show them your neck, Violet."

Her heart skipped a beat and then stuttered. Karak was right. She bore his mark. He'd given it to her against her will, but it was still there. She looked at Joss and wanted to weep. He fought against Khet and almost got away, but another of their pack brothers came in to restrain him.

"Now," Karak shrieked when she didn't comply.

"Go ahead, Violet. Show us your neck," Argram encouraged in a kind tone.

Heat flooded her cheeks as she did as her Alpha requested, baring her neck and the pale pink mark that would never fully fade. Her gaze fell to the ground as Argram came closer.

"Chin up, sister," he demanded, again in a soft tone. "You've done nothing worthy of shame."

Violet looked up, the lump in her throat that of gratitude more than fear or sorrow. She tilted her head to the side, exposing her vulnerable neck. The Alpha bent his head and took a long sniff before going back to his original position.

"Hold him tight," he told Khet and the other. Violet watched in horror as they complied, holding Joss down. "She bears Karak's mate mark."

# « CHAPTER 18 »

Joss didn't have to hear Argram's words. He'd smelled the bastard's scent on her skin the moment he'd taken her from the dilapidated shack Karak had held her in. The bite mark on her neck had been obvious. He'd not been the only one to see it. In fact, Argram had mentioned it when he'd agreed to allow her to stay in Joss's home.

That didn't stop the fury from blasting through him at the callous way the bastard was treating Violet, trying to undermine her budding confidence with a few well-placed words. He wanted to tear Karak apart right then and there. And he would have had Khet not intervened. The tips of his fingers burned as the wolf demanded freedom. Every inch of his skin stung with the prickle of fur desperate to push through the surface. The wolf demanded blood, and it would get it. He didn't care what Argram's verdict was, Karak would die.

He glanced over at Violet, who now stood a few feet to his left. Her fingers trembled as she played with the hem of her sweater, but she kept her chin up, just as the Alpha had requested. *Good.*

"Come, Violet. We're leaving," Karak demanded.

Joss growled again, showing his teeth. Soon, they would be ripping into that smug face of his.

Karak took a foolish step toward her.

"If you value your life, you will not get any closer to Violet," Argram warned.

The bastard took one look at Joss and sneered. "I want him killed for fucking my mate," he demanded.

Violet gasped, but Joss couldn't look at her. All he saw was the bastard who had hit her, assaulted her, and starved her.

"I said she bore your scent. Not that she is your mate," Argram said.

"She bears my fucking mark. She's my mate. Give her to me now." Karak's voice was rough, raspy. His frustration more evident by the constant jerky movements of his hands as he shouted the words.

"You bit her, yes. Now, show me your mate mark. Once that's confirmed, you can leave with your mate," the Alpha announced, drawing gasps from their pack mates.

"I don't have to show you a damned thing," Karak sputtered.

Joss's gaze shot to Violet. He'd never asked if she'd bitten Karak. If she had, things would be a lot more complicated to sort out. She sure as hell wasn't going back to him, but it would be harder to fight.

As soon as his gaze found hers, she shook her head, and the breath he'd been holding rushed out of his lungs.

"If you want to leave with your mate, then you will show me your mark," Argram insisted, his voice rising in anger.

"She didn't bite me," he admitted, but then gave her a wicked smile. "We were waiting until the baby arrived to make it special."

Argram turned his attention to Violet once more, who still held her head up high. "Is this true, Violet?"

She shook her head. "No, Alpha. I never claimed him because I never wanted to. He's not my mate," she said, her voice a lot stronger than Joss had expected it to be.

Karak cursed and pulled at his hair. "Don't fucking lie."

Argram growled at the man.

"She bears my mark. She comes with me," Karak stupidly insisted.

"Do you know who your mate is, Violet?" the Alpha asked, not bothering to respond to Karak.

"I do," she whispered and looked over at Joss. At that moment, Joss knew where this was heading. Violet didn't smile, but her eyes shone a little brighter. She knew it, too.

"Are you willing to give him your bite? Mark him, and claim him as your own for all the pack to see?"

Violet kept looking at him as she shook her head. "No, Alpha. I don't need to do that." A sharp gasp rushed through the crowd, and the Alpha's gaze shot to her.

Joss's heart swelled as she faced the Alpha and Karak. "I've already claimed him as my own. There is no need to bite him again."

Argram's eyes rounded, but his lips turned up the tiniest bit. "Joss, will you prove to the pack and to Karak that you are indeed claimed and have taken Violet as your mate?"

Joss tugged at his arms, releasing himself from Khet and Baron's grasps. He didn't say a word, didn't think he could with the wolf so close to the surface. Instead, he grasped his shirt and whipped it off, tossing it aside, revealing the gorgeous bite mark sitting right above his heart.

Argram came close, scenting Violet's mark and smiled. "That is Violet's mate mark. She's bitten Joss, claiming him as her own."

Karak growled. "She bears my mark. She's mine," he said through gritted teeth.

Argram stepped to the side, giving him a clear shot of Karak, but Joss held back. He waited for it. The challenge was coming, and he welcomed it.

"It doesn't matter that you've bitten her. It only matters that she has bitten Joss. She's made her choice," Argram said, his voice more menacing than it had been.

Karak's chest rose and fell in quick, harsh breaths. Hatred flashed in his eyes as he looked at Violet. "You fucking whore," he spat, then lunged at her, shifting as he did.

Material tore. His? Karak's? It didn't matter. Joss heard Violet's scream, but it was too late. Karak issued his challenge the moment he'd made a move toward her, and Joss accepted. The bastard wasn't getting away.

# « CHAPTER 19 »

Violet didn't want to watch, but she couldn't tear her gaze away. Blood covered Joss's gorgeous pelt. He leaped onto Karak, tearing into him with teeth and claws, but Karak was fast. He struck Joss's underbelly, slicing deep gouges into his flesh. Argram stood on one side of her, Wesken on the other, protecting her, yet not standing in her way.

The fine layer of sticky snow on the ground turned pink as blood spattered onto it, melting it with its warmth. Violet wanted to scream and make them stop, but a wolf challenge ended in one way. Death. The victor was the survivor. Period.

Karak managed to get his teeth into Joss's side, and Violet felt the pain inside her. Joss didn't stop, didn't slow down. For every bite and scratch Karak landed, Joss managed two. Karak scooted out of reach, panting heavily, then lunged again.

A hard tightening in her stomach made pain rip through her. She doubled over, clutching her belly. *It's too soon.*

Wesken's eyes didn't miss a thing. With a look at Khet, he sent the man scurrying.

The growls and snarls became louder as the battle drew closer. Argram stepped a little in front of her as Delana came rushing over. "What's going on?" she asked, ignoring the challenge altogether. The pack didn't have a doctor, but Delana was their healer. If nothing else, she'd have an idea of what to do.

"It's the baby, something is wrong," she gasped as the muscles tightened and twisted in her stomach.

The clearing grew silent but for Karak's snarling. Had she yelled it out? Joss looked at her, and that was all the opportunity Karak needed to jump him. In an instant, he had Joss pinned to the ground, his neck between his teeth.

"No," she screamed. Before she knew what she was doing, she took off running toward the fighting wolves, clutching at her belly. Argram was on her before she made it more than a few steps. She looked on in horror as Karak stared right at her. He shook his head—hard. Joss's head whipped from one side to the other.

Her heart stuttered, but then Joss gave a huge push with his paws, sending Karak back. The flesh of his neck gave, sending more blood splattering onto the snow, but at least he wasn't pinned down anymore.

In an instant, Joss was on him. He clamped his teeth around Karak's throat. Rather than pin him and break the wolf's neck, Joss stared into her eyes as he clamped his jaw tighter and tighter around Karak's windpipe. Karak fought against him, struggling to get out of his grasp, but Joss was too strong. Karak's movements became jerky and his eyes bulged as he tried to gasp for breath, but there was no way.

Another spasm in her stomach, stronger than the others, had her doubling over again. The fiery pain tightened her muscles and she couldn't catch her breath. She tried to look at Joss, needing his reassuring presence even if he couldn't come to her, but the world darkened around her until all went black.

***

Joss paced outside his bedroom door. Miga and Delana had gone in to check on Violet what felt like hours ago.

"Come sit, or you'll reopen your wounds." Khet tried to get him to calm down for the tenth time in half as many minutes.

"What the hell is taking so long?" he asked no one in particular.

"They just went in there. Give Delana and Miga time."

"It's been," he glanced at his watch, "eight minutes? That can't be right. My watch is wrong."

"If you don't sit down, I'm going to make you. Violet's going to be pissed if you're hurt more than you already are when you go and see her. I'm not going to be responsible for angering your new mate."

"Fuck you," he said with a growl. Of course, he didn't mean it, but cursing out his friend—and brother-in-law—was preferable to wearing a groove on the floor, or worse, bursting in there and demanding answers they couldn't yet provide.

As soon as he'd heard her frightened words about something being wrong with the baby, he'd known the battle had to end. Too bad the distraction had cost him in flesh and blood. He'd wanted to make Karak's death slow and painful, and Violet to know that the bastard would never be able to hurt her again, but when her face had paled and she'd stumbled, his heart had stopped. With one huge shake of his head, Karak's neck had snapped. He'd dropped him to the ground, but he couldn't make it to her before she fell.

Argram had scooped her up as she crumbled. "Come," Argram had ordered as he turned and carried her back to their home. Somehow, in all the commotion, Miga had been summoned to their house, as well. Being the Alpha female, she dealt with more delicate issues with the female wolves. The fact that she was a mother and might have additional insight helped, too.

Lanie came out, closing the door quietly behind her. She gave him a small smile. "Why don't you sit so I can tell you what's going on."

*Fuck no.* Joss didn't need to sit. He needed to be with Violet. No matter what they faced, they'd do it together. His chest hurt, and he clutched the spot where she'd bitten him. *She has to be okay.*

"Jesus, I said we could talk, I didn't deliver bad news," she said as she came over. "You're not going to pass out, are you? You lost a lot of blood out there."

"Fucking tell me," he demanded, not caring that he sounded like an asshole.

"She's okay—for now. The baby seems to have decided that it wanted to make an early appearance."

"He," Joss said. "Or she. Violet doesn't like for the baby to be called an it."

"Well, he or she wants out. I've given her some herbs to try to stop it, but it's not working. I think we're going to have to deliver the baby."

"It's too soon."

Lanie shook her head. "After checking her out and talking to her, I think she's closer to eight months than seven. She's small, but then she was undernourished for a lot of her pregnancy. I think the baby will be okay," she said.

"And what about Violet? How is she doing?" He hadn't had much time to adjust to the idea of being a father, but he had, and he wanted that baby as much as he would if he or she were his own. But if something happened to Violet, he didn't think he'd survive.

"She's okay, but she's scared. She's asking for you."

Before the last word was out of her mouth, Joss was down the hall and opening the door. He needed to see with his own eyes that she was okay.

As soon as she laid her eyes on him, they filled with tears. "They said the baby is coming."

Joss crossed the room and sat next to her, taking her hand in his. "That's what Delana said. I can't wait to meet him or her," he told her.

"You think everything's going to be okay?"

He leaned down and kissed her forehead, then her nose, and finally her lips. "It's going to be fine, love. We'll have to buy a bassinette for the room until we move and then get a proper crib, but that's not a problem." He knew she wasn't asking about their living arrangements, but if she suspected the worry inside him, she'd never relax enough to deliver the baby safely.

Her eyes widened. "You're right. We have nowhere for the baby to sleep."

"Don't worry. I'll ask someone to get one for us. I promise."

She closed her eyes and took a deep breath, then opened them again. "Karak?"

Joss wouldn't give the man more than a passing thought. He didn't belong in their new life. "He's dead. We don't need to think of him ever again."

She nodded and placed a hand on her belly. "Are you really okay with this? I mean, I—"

Nope. He wasn't letting her finish that sentence. "I already love our baby more than life itself, and his—or her—momma, too."

Her gaze flashed to his, and a slow smile came to her lips. "We're going to be okay?"

He grinned right back at her. "We are."

"I love you, too, Joss."

He took her cheeks between his palms and gave her a long, tender kiss.

"As much as I want more of that, I think it's going to have to wait." Her voice rose with the last of her words. "The cramps are coming back."

## « CHAPTER 20 »

Violet sat in the chair humming as she nursed Veda, rocking her back and forth. Joss sat on the bed, a huge grin on his face as he pulled the tape in place on Finn's diaper. They'd be moving into their new house later, and she couldn't wait. As much as she loved having the babies rooming with her and Joss, it did tend to put a damper on certain intimacies she was anxious to get to again now that the twins were old enough to be in their rooms.

No one had been more shocked than her when not one, but two babies had arrived. She'd been small for even a single pregnancy, never mind twins, but sure enough, as soon as Veda had made her appearance, the contractions had started again, and Finn had come wailing out.

The two months since their arrival had flown by, but she was ready to get reacquainted with her mate's body. Oh, they'd found time here and there to be with one another, thanks to Aunt Lanie, who came to steal the babies from time to time, but it wasn't nearly enough. Not for her anyway. And by the hungry looks he kept casting her way, it wasn't for Joss, either.

"As soon as she's done eating, we'll bundle them up and go to the new house. I'll have the men come for our belongings afterward," he told her as though they hadn't already had that discussion five times. She couldn't help but smile. He was so eager for the move, which in turn, had her excited, too. She couldn't wait to move in and make it theirs. The interior of the house had been finished for a few days, but Joss had wanted to be sure no paint fumes remained for the babies to breathe in. If he wasn't the postcard for the overprotective father, she didn't know who was.

Veda finally released her nipple. It took all of two seconds for Joss to place Finn gently in the bassinette and rush over. "Here, let me do that. You can go get ready," he said as he scooped Veda up, holding the baby to his shoulder as he started patting her back, coaxing the little burp from her body.

Violet stood, then reaching up onto tiptoes, she gave him a chaste kiss. "I love you, Joss."

He gave her a playful growl and leaned down to capture her lips, claiming her mouth. "I love you, too," he said when he finally released her. "Now go get ready."

She took a quick shower and dried her hair. During warmer months, she'd have let it dry on its own, but the cold winter air and the thick layer of snow covering the ground meant she had to spend a few extra minutes. But Joss never seemed to mind. He looked up at her with a smile on his face when she entered the room dressed and ready to go.

"Okay, let's get them over there before they decide they're hungry again," he said. He already had both snowsuits lined up on the bed. He placed Veda in the pink one and started bundling her up as Violet did the same for Finn in his blue suit. Their tiny hats, mittens, and booties had been gifts from Miga, who had knit them herself, and always kept their little fingers and toes warm.

As soon as she had her coat, hat, mitts, and boots on, Joss helped her with the leather carrier Wesken had made for the babies, then gently placed Veda into it, securing her against her chest. Soon Finn was strapped to Joss, and they were heading out the door.

"It's a beautiful day," she exclaimed as she walked out. The sun shone through the trees, making the fresh snow that had fallen the day before sparkle. Her breath puffed out in a white cloud in front of her face.

"Yes, it is." He took her hand as they started walking.

Violet looked around and giggled. "We're going in the wrong direction," she told him about halfway down the block.

He grinned at her. "We have to stop at Delana's first. Is that okay?" he asked, a devilish glint in his eyes.

"What are you up to, Joss?"

He kissed her nose and tugged on her hand. "You'll see."

Whatever it was, she was sure she'd love it. Joss surprised her with gifts and his brand of sweetness all the time. And she'd never tire of it.

As soon as they came walking up the step to Khet and Delana's house, the front door swung open. Delana stood there with a huge smile on her face. "It's about time you two showed up," she huffed good-naturedly.

"Hi, Delana," Violet said as she climbed the steps.

"What, you're not going to say hello to your sister?" Zeyde stood in the doorway, a huge smile on her face. "What are you waiting for? I haven't seen my niece and nephew in close to a month. Lanie says we have babysitting duties tonight."

Violet looked over her shoulder at Joss, who smiled and walked up behind her.

"Babysitting duties?" she asked as she gave her sister as tight a hug as she could manage with a baby strapped to her chest.

"Oh, that's right. That was a secret, wasn't it? Oops. Sorry, Joss."

Delana laughed and ushered them all inside. "Okay, I have all the milk I'll need in the fridge. We have diapers, little bitty baby clothes, and the bassinettes should get here soon. Time for you guys to leave," she said without hesitation.

Violet opened her mouth to protest, but Zeyde was already unbuckling the carrier from around her. Delana was doing the same, taking Finn from Joss.

"Have fun, guys," Zeyde said in a singsong voice, but she then gave an exaggerated sigh. "Okay, kiss them good-bye first if you must, but then it's time to go."

Already Delana had Finn out of his gear and was making cooing noises at him. "Say bye DaDa. Bye, Momma." Finn blew a spit bubble at his aunt, totally uninterested in his parents' departure.

In a manner of minutes, Violet found herself outside again, two babies shy of a full family, and swept off her feet. Joss spun her around and around, laughing at her high-pitched squeal. When they finally stopped, he captured her mouth with his, devouring her as though he'd never had a taste before and never would again.

"We can come back for them before nightfall if you can't stand being away from them for so long," he said when he finally released her lips.

She gave him a playful nip, then kissed him again. "Let's go home, Joss," she said. She had no idea if she'd last all night without the babies close by, but she'd take advantage of every moment alone with her mate until then.

Grasping Joss's hand, she ran down the sidewalk, passing Khet and Rennan along the way. They each carried a bassinette. "Thank you," Joss called out as he followed. They'd stop and talk another time. Right then, they had more important things to do.

# « CHAPTER 21 »

Joss opened the door, then stepped back for Violet to walk into their new home. The light scent of melted wax drifted out. He'd been tempted to fill the whole house with candles, but he wasn't sure how long the smell would last or if it was good for the babies, so he'd settled for a few in the master bedroom. He'd open the windows before they left to collect Veda and Finn to make sure the room aired out.

Violet gasped and covered her mouth with her hands. Her eyes shone brightly as she took in the pine tree he'd chopped down and had Delana decorate for them in the foyer. Of course, there'd be another in the family room, one they could decorate as a family next week before the holiday, but he'd wanted to surprise her with this one.

Violet shook her head and smiled at him before going into the family room to the right. Joss held his breath. If there was anything she didn't like, they'd change it. He'd have to figure out how to do it with them living there. Already plans were in effect to remodel his old house to accommodate two of the women displaced from the Mahehkan pack, and work was scheduled to begin tomorrow.

"It's even better than I imagined it would be," Violet exclaimed before she threw herself into his arms.

"Are you sure? We can change things." Violet had been an active participant in choosing colors, materials, and furnishings, but he hadn't let her see the finished product. Partly because he wanted her to see it after it was all done, but mostly because he hadn't wanted her breathing in the construction fumes.

She rained kisses all over his face and neck before giggling and pulling back. "Of course, I haven't seen everything, but I'm sure I'll love the other rooms, too."

He gave her a warning growl as she stepped away from him. "Want the tour?"

Violet grinned up at him as she pulled her coat off and hung it on the banister before yanking her sweater over her head and setting it on top. "Only if the tour starts in our bedroom," she said breathlessly as she turned and dashed up the stairs.

Joss watched, enjoying the view as she ran. By the time he reached the bedroom, her bra was on the chair, and she was pulling her jeans off her foot. All that was left was a little bit of white lace, covering her while not hiding a single thing.

"Damn, you're stunning," he said as he stalked closer.

Cheeks stained pink, her gaze met his, stopping him in his tracks. Violet pulled her hair over her right shoulder, then pointed to a spot right above her left breast.

Joss's heart pounded.

"Do you know what this is?" she asked him, her voice soft.

All the moisture in his mouth disappeared. Unable to speak, he shook his head. He knew what he wanted it to be, but he wouldn't assume.

"That's the spot I want you to bite me, Joss. I want your mark. Right there, above my heart. Will you give it to me?" she asked as she trailed her fingertip from that spot down her breast, and over her already taut nipple.

Joss had hoped that the day when she'd allow him to make her his would come soon, but she'd never mentioned it, and he hadn't asked. When the time was right, he knew it would happen, and he'd contented himself with that. But hearing her words, seeing the love shining in her eyes, it was almost more than he could bear.

He closed the distance between them and took her lips in a tender kiss. "Nothing would make me happier, love," he said, his voice thick.

She dug her fingers into his hair, pulling him close and claiming his mouth. Her tongue darted out, demanding entrance. He opened up to her, moaning. She rubbed her body against his, her nipples grazing his chest, her hips wreaking havoc with his already engorged cock.

By the time she released him again, he couldn't think past the haze of lust pounding through him. His cock, hard and heavy, strained against his zipper.

"You need to get rid of your clothes," she said. Her chest rose and fell with her quick breaths, drawing his gaze to her breasts.

Joss grabbed his shirt at the back between his shoulder blades with one hand and yanked it off. Before he could reach for his belt, she was there. She made quick work of unfastening it, then popped the snap.

He loved when she took the lead, allowing her needs to come first. It proved how far she'd come. He couldn't say the mild female he'd rescued was gone, but she sure as hell wasn't in the bedroom. His zipper came down with a rasp, and he held his breath.

A moment later, she freed his cock and wrapped her fingers around the shaft. Heated pleasure rushed through him at her simple touch. The slow glide from root to tip had him moaning and thrusting into her palm.

Not wanting to waste a moment of their time together, he pushed his jeans down past his hips even as she stroked him. As amazing as her hand was, he wanted more—needed more.

Grabbing her by the waist, he lifted Violet to him. As soon as he did, she had her legs wrapped around his waist. He moaned at the soft rub of lace against his shaft as he pressed against her. "I want you, Violet. Right now."

"Yes. Now," Violet panted next to his ear before nipping Joss's neck. Her teeth on his skin sent more pleasure rippling through him.

"How much do you love these panties?" he asked even as he grasped the material on either side of her hips.

She pulled back and grinned down at him. "A lot, but not nearly as much as I love you."

"I'll buy you more," he said as he gave a little tug. The scrap of material slipped off Violet's body and down to the floor.

Joss stepped out of his pants, leaving them behind as he took Violet to the bed. Her hands were in his hair again, making his cock throb with the little pulls on his scalp. She writhed against him, rubbing herself on his shaft. He leaned over, intent on laying her on the bed, then grinned at her lusty growl. "I want to savor this moment, love," he said in the way of explanation.

This time, when he leaned forward, she released him, looking up at him with her eyes half closed and her lip caught between her teeth. She brought her hands to her breasts, cupping them, then tugging on her nipples as he watched.

Moaning, he leaned forward and flicked his tongue over first one peak, then the other. When she would have reached for his hair again, he kissed a trail down her belly.

He looked up at her from his position between her legs, his mouth poised just out of reach. "I can't wait to hear you scream, Violet."

Before she could say anything at all, he lowered his head. He licked all the way down her slit and up again, gathering her essence, taking it for himself.

She moaned and thrust her pelvis higher.

Gripping her hips, he held her steady as he tasted every part of her, dipping his tongue into her heated pussy, then licking and sucking on her clit until she writhed against his mouth. Her moans and sighs grew louder, and her hands found his hair again as she held him where she wanted him, but then an instant later, she stiffened and released him.

Shocked by the sudden change, Joss stopped and looked up at her.

"Not now," she said as she took big gulps of air. "I don't want to come yet. I want you inside me. I want you to bite me. Make me yours," she panted.

He climbed over her and rested the bulk of his weight on his forearms. His heart pounded as he positioned himself at her entrance. With the candle light playing on her skin, her lips puffy from his kisses, and the love shining back at him in her eyes, she looked like an angel. So fucking beautiful.

Claiming her mouth, he sank into her, not stopping until he filled her. When he withdrew and slid back in, she tried to thrust up and take more of him than he was willing to give her, and he growled. The sound had her pussy clenching around him and her nipples tightening against his chest, so he did it again. Her hot grip made him moan right along with her.

He continued to plunge deep inside her as he kissed his way along her jaw and down to her right shoulder. He nipped her skin there before moving on to her breast. He licked a slow circle around her nipple, then sucked it between his lips.

She tunneled her fingers into his hair again, holding him as he continued his onslaught. Each thrust of his hips had another moan, longer and louder than the last, slipping past her lips. His cock ached, and his balls drew up tight.

When he didn't think either of them could take any more, he released her and moved to the left. He flicked his tongue over the hard peak until she was chanting his name and the muscles in her pussy tightened around him.

He lifted his gaze to hers, finding her watching him with nothing but love and adoration shining in her eyes. Violet held her breath when he kissed the spot right above her heart.

Joss quickened his thrusts, filling her with long, hard strokes. He scraped his teeth over her skin, teasing her. When he gave her a small nip, her eyes rolled a little as her pussy fluttered around him.

"Yes, please, now, Joss," she begged.

Unable to deny her, he did as she asked, biting into her soft flesh, marking not only her skin but her very soul. Violet threw her head back and screamed out his name as her pussy clenched and released around him.

He thrust into her, drawing out her pleasure until he couldn't hold back. He came with a shout and stilled, emptying himself deep inside his mate.

The faint coppery taste of her blood lingered on his tongue from the bite he'd given her. He nuzzled the spot gently, in case it was sore. She was his. In all ways possible.

Violet wiggled beneath him.

"Are you okay?" he asked as realization set in that he was crushing her with his weight.

He tried to move to her side, but she grinned as she resisted. "Never better."

Even though she tried to hold him where he was, he flipped so that she was on top of him. "Isn't that better?"

She giggled. "Maybe. I guess breathing is a good thing," she said as she nuzzled his neck, then nipped at the mating mark she'd given him the first time they'd made love.

"*You're* a good thing. A very good thing," Joss insisted.

She looked up at him, her eyes wide. "Are we really leaving the babies over at Delana's all night?"

"I asked them to keep them for the night, but they expect us after dinner," he said, grinning when her smile brightened.

"That's not for another four hours," she said as she licked the spot above his heart.

He nodded. "Maybe we're not ready for a whole night without them, but I'm sure we can find something to occupy us for a few more hours," he said, stroking a hand down her spine.

She gave him a sexy grin. "Oh, I have plenty of ideas," she said before she kissed him.

http://elianneadams.com/

For the most up to date information about new releases subscribe to my Newsletter.

> Online: www.elianneadams.com
> On Facebook: Élianne Adams
> On Twitter: @ÉlianneAdams

I love to hear from readers. If you enjoyed Lost in Magic, please leave a review at Amazon.com or Goodreads.com. Your feedback is invaluable to make the stories what they are.

Élianne Adams

http://elianneadams.com/

## About the Author

Born of snow and ice, or at least near snow and ice in North Eastern Ontario, Canada, Élianne Adams has always enjoyed curling up with a good book and a warm blanket. Even before she really knew what love was, she dreamed of writing her own happily ever after stories. It wasn't until her very own hero encouraged her to follow her lifelong dream that she began putting the words begging to be told onto the page. When she isn't reading or writing, Élianne can be found spending time with her husband, three children and pets.

www.ingramcontent.com/pod-product-compliance
Lightning Source LLC
Chambersburg PA
CBHW021157130626
46554CB00005B/1860